"Hi, you made it." She was waiting outside the entrance to radiology, relief beaming out of those beautiful eyes.

And drilling into his gut. Reminding him of how well they fit together. Not only physically but they seemed to agree on the most important things. Suddenly the stress of getting here, of even having to be here, fell away and he reached for her hand. "Let's go do this." He wanted the first glimpse of his son or daughter more than anything.

Her fingers slipped between his; warm, soft, Alesha.

"Now there's a surprise." The girl pushing her scanner into Alesha's stomach grinned. "There are two in there."

"What?" The word exploded out of Kristof. "Twins?"

"Two?" squeaked a stunned Alesha. "Two babies. Oh my."

Dear Reader,

Earlier this year I went to Dubrovnik with my husband for a few nights. What a beautiful place and we didn't want to leave. On our first night staying in an apartment we got locked out in very similar fashion to Alesha Milligan, and immediately I knew how my next story was going to start.

I had a lot of fun putting Alesha and Kristof Montfort together in this wonderful setting. One week can make a huge difference to people's lives and that's what happens to these two. Of course nothing goes to plan, there are always hiccups on the way to true love and we have to go to London to sort these two out.

I hope you enjoy a taste of Dubrovnik as you follow Alesha and Kristof as they fall in love and begin to find a way to make it all work—forever.

Cheers,

Sue MacKay

sue.mackay56@yahoo.com
suemackay.co.nz

SURPRISE TWINS
FOR THE SURGEON

———

SUE MacKAY

HARLEQUIN® MEDICAL ROMANCE™

Recycling programs
for this product may
not exist in your area.

ISBN-13: 978-1-335-66367-2

Surprise Twins for the Surgeon

First North American Publication 2018

Copyright © 2018 by Sue MacKay

Printed in U.S.A.

To all my wonderful readers. Without you
I wouldn't have this wonderful career.

CHAPTER ONE

'IT'S PERFECT.' Or it would've been. Alesha Milligan spun around on her toes, arms wide as she scoped the spacious apartment she was going to spend the next week enjoying. She *would* enjoy it. *Thank you very much, Luke.* Her arms fell to her sides, her chin dropped, and all pretence at how exciting a holiday in Dubrovnik would be evaporated.

This was supposed to be seven whole, luxurious days and nights seeing the sights, hitting the clubs, forgetting all about work and patients, having an amazing time with Luke. Instead she was here alone, dumped a fortnight ago. He apparently was now headed for Paris instead of Croatia as they'd planned. Her stomach squeezed painfully. Paris where he was hooking up with another woman he'd met at an accountants' conference last month.

'Hope it rains every day in Paris.'

'Pardon?' The proprietor, who'd introduced

herself as Karolina, looked concerned. As if she'd let her apartment to a madwoman.

'Sorry. I was meant to be here with a man, only he changed his mind.' Should've seen it coming. It wasn't as though she was a stranger to men cooling towards her just when she finally relaxed into a relationship and Luke hadn't exactly been rushing to spend time with her every night lately.

Karolina's face fell. 'That's terrible. You still want to stay?'

She was here, wasn't she? If she went home she wouldn't be able to face her girlfriends after all their nagging for her to go to Dubrovnik and have a great time despite Luke. Cherry had even had the audacity to suggest she have a sizzling fling, burn out the angst in her veins. Her? Sex with another man other than Luke? She wasn't ready. That'd make her seem fickle, and fickle she wasn't. Desperate for love, yes. She was all of that, and once again had tried too hard and set herself up to be dumped. And now here she was. Alone. Might as well soak up the sun lazing by that beautiful pool beckoning from metres away on the vast deck the apartment opened onto. Throw in some sightseeing. Alone.

'Yes. I do.' If right this moment she wanted to run for the hills she could see in the distance, common sense would soon prevail and she'd make the most of this opportunity to learn something about another country she'd always wanted to visit. Finding a smile for Karolina wasn't easy, but slowly her lips tipped upward. None of this was her hostess's fault. 'You have a beautiful spot here.'

'Glad you're happy with it.' The tension that had started racking up in the other woman backed off and she pointed to an expensive bottle of champagne on the table. 'There's wine for you to drink.'

Alesha's smile widened. There were some things on her side, then. Luke was so tight he must've forgotten to cancel that. If she knew where he was staying in Paris she'd send him a bottle of lemon juice, no sugar added. This wouldn't have been a gesture brought on by guilt. He'd been in a hurry to get rid of her, saying the accountant he'd hooked up with was *the one*. At least he hadn't demanded she reimburse him for his share of this accommodation. Was it possible it was a consolation prize in his mind? It hadn't worked, but, yes, 'I'm going to enjoy it.' Mouthful by delicious mouthful, swallowing the anger and disappointment that was her latest ex, she would enjoy it as a precursor to having a wonderful holiday.

A holiday alone. Pain blurred her sight, removed her smile. What was wrong with her that men didn't stay around for ever? Not only men. Her parents hadn't either.

'There are plastic glasses in that cupboard if you want to enjoy a drink by the pool.'

Alesha snatched up the bottle, ready for a glass now. 'It should be in the fridge.' And she should be acting outwardly strong, if broken on the inside. After all, it wasn't as though this had never happened to her before. Not a cancelled romantic holiday. *That* was new, but broken relationships were becoming her speciality.

'I want you to have a lovely stay. There is a lot to do in and around Dubrovnik.' Karolina handed her a card. 'If there's anything you need, call me. I recommend you put my number on your phone. I don't live on the premises but I'm available any time.'

'Will do.' Alesha slid the card into her shorts' pocket. She'd deal with that shortly. First she'd go stick her toes in that sparkling, crystal-clear water.

Karolina removed a metal ring from the door, and waved keys at her. 'Front door, laundry, and the gate off the street, which must be kept locked at all times for everyone's security.'

'No problem.' They also went into her pocket. 'Do you have a map of the town?'

'All the information you'll need is on that shelf above the table. Restaurants and grocery shops are highlighted. Bus stops, the way to the Old City if you want to walk. Anything else just ask around. Most locals are very friendly.'

'I will, and thanks. I am going to have a wonderful time.' She really was, as soon as she'd banished Luke's haughty face from behind her eyelids. Haughty? Yes, he had been, especially as he'd said she'd got too serious too soon. Hello? Hadn't he also said he'd fallen for the accountant woman instantly? Alesha's stomach tightened. He could've just said it wasn't working for him, not layer in how wonderful this other woman was—at everything.

A bird tweet in her pocket had her tugging her phone out fast. He'd changed his mind.

He hadn't.

'Hi, Cherry. You on break?' She wandered out to the pool's edge as she listened to her friend back in London.

'No, but I wanted to give you the heads up. There's a six-month position coming up on the paediatric ward starting in four weeks. One of the nurses is taking maternity leave, but she's told me it's unlikely she'll come back at all. This'd be the ideal job for you. I've flicked the application form through to your email.'

A couple of weeks ago she'd have jumped

at the opportunity. Probably still would once her head and bruised heart settled back into the 'being single' groove. But right now? Alesha didn't want to make any plans for the future other than getting out of bed every morning to go discover this wonderland. 'Thanks for letting me know. I'll think about it over the next few days.'

'Don't take too long. Rumour has it nurses from all over London will be queuing up for the chance to join our team. It'd be cool to work together. So, how's Dubrovnik?'

Alesha hadn't really taken much in yet—she had been too busy feeling sorry for herself on the drive from the airport, instead thinking Luke should've been with her. Wandering over to the wall at the front of the deck, she stared out and around. 'It's beautiful,' she gasped. 'There's an awesome bridge in the background, and hills, and almost right beneath where I'm standing is the harbour where the cruise ships tie up.'

'There'll be nightclubs and the like there, surely? You can be out all night, and lounging by the pool during the day.' Cherry sounded excited for her.

Down, girl. 'Yeah, well, I'm sure there'll be some dancing and drinking going on. Not so sure about having that fling though. I do know there're lots of places I want to visit during the day.'

'You Kiwis and your sightseeing. Can't you visit a town without spending the days walking for miles, taking photos and making yourself too tired to go out at night?' Cherry laughed. 'Oh-oh, dragon on the warpath. Got to go. Put your CV in for that job. Bye.'

Click. Gone.

Alesha sank onto a lounger. The heat was softening her muscles, moistening her skin, draining what little energy she had left. The temptation to fall into the water fully clothed was strong. *There's a phone in my pocket.* Could remove it, but if she was going to do that she might as well get into her bikini. The tiny red creation made to cover the essentials and cause havoc in a man's brain. In his shorts. Instead she'd wear it for a swim on her own. She'd also pour a glass of bubbles as soon as they were remotely chilled. Right about now.

Dressed, make that just decent, in her new bikini and with a glass of lukewarm champagne, Alesha tossed her phone on the bed and returned to the poolside to stretch out on the lounger to soak up some sun. Already hot, it was nice to feel the heat pushing her down into the cushions. Talk about the life. If she had to be alone then this was the way to go.

How some fun, maybe get laid. Put Luke behind you. He doesn't deserve you anyway.

Leap into bed with just any guy she met? As if she were a tramp? Would that make her a more interesting person? When she'd be uptight and stressed about meeting men in bars on her own? They'd have a different agenda from hers. Theirs would be to head straight to bed, while she was far more cautious. If that made her dull, then dull she was.

I can't deal with this. I've been dumped. Like yesterday's news. A fling doesn't require getting to know the other person too much.

Forget the fling and just have fun doing the things she enjoyed.

I enjoy sex.

The thought made her start. Sitting up, she stared around the beautiful complex with its stunning pool. Was she broken-hearted over Luke's defection? Or hurt because once again she'd failed to find love?

So? It wasn't as if she were incapacitated. Basically she was used to being on her own. Alesha hadn't moved all the way from the other side of the world because she was a wuss. No, she'd shifted to a humongous city where she knew no one, had found jobs, accommodation, a man who'd enjoyed her company for the past few months—or so she'd thought.

Her hands clenched as sweat trickled between her breasts, down her back. The sun beat down relentlessly, heating her skin while internally her blood was frozen and her stomach a lump of ice. Love was an intangible, and always out of her reach. She'd been searching for love since the day her brother got sick and her parents no longer had time for her. She'd been trying too hard to be loved by someone special. It might be time to accept it wasn't going to happen and she should just get on with her life. Get busy so she didn't notice no one was there for her, with her.

Or maybe she should relax, have some uncomplicated fun as Cherry and Shelley suggested and see where that took her.

Alesha gulped a mouthful of champagne, spluttered as it went down the wrong way.

Stop feeling sorry for yourself.

'Yeah,' she sighed. She did have a darned good life living in London, sharing a house with other nurses she got on well with and often contracted to work in some of the best hospitals. Much more exciting and interesting than living in Christchurch, New Zealand, where she'd grown up.

Taking a small sip of the champagne this time, she groaned out loud in exasperation. Her clenched hand pounded the mattress at her side. What a fantastic way to start a holiday. She was not going to spend the week lying on the bed feeling sorry for herself. She *was* not.

Okay. Message received. She'd start enjoying the sun, the blue sky that went for ever, the view of hills and the harbour below. Even the champagne that in all honesty wasn't flash in its warmish state. There was a whole world out there waiting to be explored. Alesha would not leave here next weekend without knowing the sights and sounds and smells of Dubrovnik. But first she was going to get into that pool and cool off, physically and mentally. Then she'd go for a walk and see what was nearby for eating out. If her appetite returned by the end of the week, that was.

Luke could go to hell in a wheelbarrow. A rusty one with a flat tyre. There were other men out there.

Exhaustion pulled at her.

A sad sigh escaped. She would have a great time despite going solo. She really, really would, as soon as she'd had a snooze. Yeah, sure. Her eyes stung, proving she wasn't quite ready to let go the hurt. But crying was not happening. Rarely since the day when she was ten, and stood at her brother's graveside to drop onto the coffin the silver clock shaped like a Labrador and small enough to fit in the palm of Ryan's hand, had Alesha given into tears. The clock had been bought out of hard-earned pocket money mowing lawns for Dad and the people next door. Ryan had been meant to get better and take it with him wherever he went in the future.

She laid back and closed her eyes, savouring the sun as she'd done so often on family holidays a good many years ago. Sun, sea, surf. It was what Kiwis made the most of every summer around Christmas and New Year. A relaxed, exciting time with family and friends, just mucking about in the water, catching fish…

A light breeze tightened her skin. Alesha dragged her eyes open and rolled onto her back. 'Ouch.' Sitting up, she looked over her shoulder, got an eyeful of red skin. The tube of sunscreen was still inside her case. Probably where her brain was too. Protecting her skin from the sun was always a priority. Not today. The sun was disappearing behind the hills. And she'd wasted the afternoon getting sunburnt.

A gust of wind swished across the pool and deck, and behind her a door slammed. Her fiery skin was intensely cold for a moment then back to flaming. She shivered. Time to put on some clothes.

That door that banged shut must've been hers. But it was all right. It wouldn't be locked. Not when she stood in her bikini with only a towel to wrap around her and the keys still in the pocket of her shorts lying on the floor inside.

The door didn't budge when she turned the handle, nor when she pressed a shoulder against the wood. Seriously? No way. Someone was playing a joke on her.

She was not locked out of her apartment without clothes, money or her phone. When her stomach was complaining about lack of food. Her day had just gone from average to worse. What else could go wrong? Tipping her head back, Alesha made to shout her frustration, but hauled on the brakes at the last second. What was the point? Screaming wouldn't miraculously unlock the door, or hand her phone over with Karolina's number. Had she got around to putting the woman's number in her database? She couldn't remember. Too much emotion had been whirling around in her mind.

Looking up at the apartment above, Alesha saw a light on in the lounge. Relief was instant. Whoever was in there would have the phone number she needed to resolve this glitch.

Loud knocking on that door brought no more success than trying to open her own. The light was on but no one was home. Nor was there anyone in the other apartments when she banged on their doors. Seemed she wasn't only alone but she might be sleeping on the lounger if she didn't find a way of contacting Karolina.

This would be hilarious if it hadn't happened to her. It might even be funny in a few days' time when she recounted it to her flatmates back in London, but right now it was downright scary. Another shiver wracked her while her sunburnt skin burned and chilled equally. 'I can't sleep outside.' Her stomach rumbled. 'Yeah, and you can wait and all. There's no dinner coming your way until this is sorted.'

Looking around the complex, she smothered the panic threatening to overwhelm her. Think. She was safe in here, cold and hungry, yes, but no one was going to get through the outside door leading from the road. Waiting until other guests came home was her only option, although who knew when that would be? Down on the narrow road cars went by slowly. From the far end of the pool she stared out at the view, which would have looked beautiful if she weren't just a tiny bit afraid she was going to spend the whole night out here.

Lights flickered on in the next-door house. Of course. Neighbours.

Wrapping the towel tight around her, she

headed for the gate and out onto the footpath. The gate snipped shut behind her. Her stomach nudged her toes. How stupid could she get? She was out on the street in a bikini and it was getting dark. Lying on the lounger by the pool all night suddenly seemed almost like fun.

Neighbours, remember. Someone would know the owner of the apartments. They had to.

They might've but they didn't speak English. No one at the four houses she tried understood a word she said; instead they looked at her as though she was a madwoman gibbering away in a foreign language—she was fast approaching becoming one—and closed their doors in her face. She should've learnt a few more words of Croatian other than hello and thank you, though it would never have occurred to her to learn 'how do I get in touch with Karolina?' or 'I need a locksmith'.

Back on the street Alesha blinked away the irritant in her eyes. Crying was not happening. This was a holiday, shambolic yes, but a holiday in a beautiful place, and meant to be enjoyed. All she had to do was find a way back into her apartment. How hard could it be?

A couple was walking up the road, talking and laughing.

Relief lifted her heart. 'Hello. Do you speak English? Can you help me, please?'

They did stop and look at her, before shaking their heads in bewilderment and carrying on up the hill.

That had to be a no, then.

A woman came around the corner, a phone plastered to her ear.

'Excuse me. Do you speak English?'

Apparently not. The woman didn't even slow down.

Alesha walked down the road a hundred metres, asking everyone she saw the same questions, getting the same result.

The night stretched ahead interminably. What she wouldn't give to be back in her flat eating yesterday's leftovers and throwing darts at the board after she'd pinned a photo of Luke to it. It had all started with him, hadn't it?

No, it went way further back than him.

Kristof Montfort strolled up the hill, hands in pockets, glad the day was done and the temperature was dropping to something near bearable. Once in a rare year London might get as hot. Might. A cold beer beckoned, and his feet moved faster.

The little girl found curled up, shivering, in the bushes by the Dubrovnik Bridge had been brought in to his mother at the Croatian Children's Home during the night and had stolen into his heart when he hadn't been looking as he worked with her. He must be getting soft because the tiny child's big fear-filled eyes, her gaunt cheeks, and scrawny body had angered him, destroyed his usually well-controlled emotions and let her in where he never let anyone. It had taken all day to get his equilibrium back. How could a parent abandon their child to the vagaries of street thieves and child porn operators? His father might've made a mockery of all he taught Kristof about being an honest, reputable gentleman, but he'd never physically hurt him, and the emotional slam dunk had happened when he was old enough to fend for himself.

They were yet to learn the child's name so in the meantime everyone was calling her Capeka—little stork—for her inclination to stand on one leg with the other twisted behind her knee as she huddled in a corner.

He'd done all he could for Capeka today; operating to fix an arm with multiple fractures, stitching deep, badly infected cuts on her thighs and forearms, putting her back together physically. Food, clean clothes and a warm bed had been priorities. The mental stuff would be taken care of by his mother and her colleagues, and would take a lot longer to resolve, if ever. The counsellors and the nurses at the Croatian Children's Home spent hours with their little patients and lost souls, but there was a gross shortage of caring nurses, the pay being minimum on a good day. Even the most fervent care-giver had to eat and find shelter and wear clothes.

'Excuse me.' A young woman dressed in a towel appeared in front of him, looking wary although desperation was rippling off her.

'Yes?'

'You speak English?' Surprise warred with disbelief.

'I am English.' And Croatian, but that was another story. 'What's your problem?' There went that cold beer. Somehow he just knew this wasn't going to be a quick question and answer session. There was something about those earthy coloured eyes that strummed him, and warned him. The woman was in trouble.

Or *was* trouble.

She jerked a thumb over her shoulder. 'I've gone and got myself locked out of the apartment I'm staying in. As well as the complex,' she added in a rush. 'I need to get hold of the owner but I don't have a phone.' Her cheeks pinked. 'Or her number.'

'You'd be talking about Karolina.'

Hope flared. 'You know her?'

He didn't want to dampen that hope; it made her look less drawn, beautiful even. 'A little, but, better than that, my mother is friends with Karolina's.' Tapping his mother's number, he held his phone to his ear. He listened to the dial tone while studying the woman before him. Temptation in a towel. 'Fingers crossed my mother has her phone with her. She has a habit of leaving it all over town.'

Her shoulders drooped. 'Oh.'

'Is that you, Kristof?'

Kristof raised a thumb in his distraction's direction. 'Yes, Mum, it's me. And before you start in on me about not taking a partner to the fundraiser dinner tomorrow, I've got someone here who's got herself locked out of the Jelinski Apartments and needs to get in touch with Karolina.' As in the lady he was *not* taking to the dinner even if his mother had begged him to.

'She came here to pick up her mother and left five minutes ago. I've tried to give you Karolina's number so many times.'

So you have. Your persistence is admirable, but please use it on more important issues.

He liked Karolina. He didn't have the hots for her, or love her, or want to get to know her better, though he'd do anything for her if she asked because that was who he was these days, and she felt the same about him. Though she might not do anything he asked. Their respective mothers had other ideas and wouldn't listen to them. What did they know? Kristof's mother, in particular, refused to accept that he'd decided not to marry again, ever. Why would he when his ex-wife had cheated on him more times than he could count? Had laughed when he'd told her he loved her and that monogamy was part of their relationship. A deal breaker for him, but her idea of love included adventurous affairs on the side.

The woman before him was looking at him as though he was her saviour, and shivering, wrapped only in that towel and who knew what underneath? Nothing? 'Mum, please let Karolina know she's needed at the apartments urgently.'

Now he noticed red, string-like straps running over her shoulders. A bikini? Or a bra? Whichever, no better than nothing for warmth. But slightly easier on his overactive libido, which did not have a role to play here. It might've been a few months since he'd seen to that need but he would not be scratching it with this woman, despite the heat starting to flow into his blood. Shoving the phone into his back pocket, he told her, 'You shouldn't have to wait long. Karolina lives four streets over.' As long as she'd gone straight home after dropping her mother off.

'Thanks so much. I appreciate your help. I was beginning to think I'd be spending the night out here and there's nothing other than cold concrete or tarmac.' Now that her problem was being fixed her mouth lifted into an ironic smile. 'It's been one of those days.'

Don't smile at me like that. It goes straight to places I don't want to acknowledge.

That bow-shaped upper lip and full lower one would be magic on his skin. He slapped his hand against his thigh, instantly regretting the action when she jerked backwards. 'Well, we've dealt with this problem. Glad I came along.' He was off the hook, had helped her out of a bind and could walk on with a clear conscience. Couldn't he? Kristof sucked in a breath. She wasn't as young as he'd first thought. Mid-twenties? Older? What did it matter? He wasn't interested. It was time for that beer and to forget a particularly difficult day dealing with Capeka. But his hormones got in the way and he asked, 'Why are you cold when the temperature is still warm?'

'I fell asleep by the pool for a little while and got some sunburn. Now my skin is fluctuating between hot and cold.'

Kristof looked over her shoulder and whistled. 'That's going to sting under the shower.' An image filled his brain of her tall, slim body under the water. He wasn't seeing red, more cream-coloured skin and lots of curves. Forget an itch. Muscles tightened in places they had no right.

His phone rang. Relief at the interruption was quick but didn't loosen the tension plaguing him. 'Mum? Don't tell me you couldn't get hold of Karolina?' His eyes were fixed on the woman in front of him so he didn't miss the way her body momentarily folded inward.

When she saw him watching she was quick to straighten to full height, bringing the top of her head to align with his chin, while struggling to banish the disappointment sparking in her eyes.

His mother harrumphed. 'Of course I did. Karolina will be at least half an hour though. It's something unavoidable.' In other words don't ask.

He wouldn't. 'Okay. I'll tell—' What was her name? They hadn't got around to introducing themselves. He almost didn't want to in case that made her real. Huh? How not real was this stunning female? 'We'll be waiting.' There went that beer. He explained the situation to the woman. 'By the way, I'm Kristof

Montfort.' He held his hand out. 'I'm a doctor from London over here helping my mother for a week.' That was added to reassure her he wasn't an axe murderer, not to show off. He didn't need to tell her he owed his mother for hurting her for many years. That was his guilt, not to be shared.

She put her slim hand out to shake his and the towel slid to the ground, giving him an eyeful of her body. Definitely lots of enticing curves and her skin was creamy and smooth. Got that right, then. The moisture on his tongue dried. Her breasts more than filled the ridiculously small red-and-white-fabric cups supposedly holding them in place. He couldn't breathe. Or move. But his eyes roamed. She was a stunner. From top to toes. His eyes cruised down her legs to those toes just to make sure he was right. Of course he was. This woman was hot, beautiful, a magnet for his manhood. He stepped back. Away from temptation. She'd have him locked up in a flash if he acted on the heat ramping through his body, language difficulties or not. Why had he gone and said he was hanging around until Karolina turned up?

Snatching her hand free, she bent to retrieve her only cover, quickly tying it back in place.

'Alesha Milligan, fool extraordinaire. I can't believe I left my phone and keys inside.'

'Pleased to meet you.'

Then she smiled, reminding him of sunny days on the briny in his runabout, and his stomach hit his feet. Her voice was so feminine and warm. 'Actually I'm lying. Yes, I can believe it. I'd been distracted big time. It's a surprise I remembered to take a towel outside.'

It would've been better for him if she'd remembered to take her clothes out to the poolside. Of course only someone who knew they were going to lock themselves outside would do that. 'We all stuff up at times.' As he was now, with his body still reminding him that all parts below his belt were in full working order, despite a recent lack of practice due to long hours working at the private practice in Harley Street hindering a social life. But he had to be grateful for towels. The one wound around that exquisite body was hiding even the curves. Except now he knew what was under there. Knew, and wanted another glimpse, wanted to touch and get to know.

No, he did not.

'Feel like a beer while you wait?' At least that would mean a quick break while he went home to get said liquid libation.

Her scrutiny of him seemed haughty. 'You

don't appear to have any with you and as I don't intend going to a bar dressed like this I'll say no. B-but thank you for offering.' The shivering was back, her skin lifting in goose-bumps.

Inviting her back to the house might be kinder than letting her stand out here, but then they wouldn't know when Karolina turned up. Also, his mother was still at the children's home so there was no one else at the house. Alesha might not feel comfortable spending time alone with a stranger while dressed in next to nothing. 'Give me five and I'll be back with beer and a jersey and some pants to keep you warm. They'll be too big but better than nothing.' And just might make that amazing body look as if it were hanging out in a sack.

But you'd still know what was in the sack.

Again surprise appeared in her face. Kristof liked surprising her for some reason. Maybe because green flecks appeared in the brown of her eyes? 'Th-thanks, I'd appreciate that.'

'If you're sure you're all right, I'll go now.' She'd be safe but not comfortable. He'd be fast. She was also a visitor to his second country, and visitors were meant to be treated kindly. Yes, that was what this was all about. Taking care of a visitor. Nothing to do with this hissing and fizzing in his veins. 'Be right back.'

He'd have that flare of excitement going on in his groin under control by the time he returned. Hopefully hanging out here in the dark only lightened by low-quality street lamps he'd be safe from those deep, alluring pools blinking at him from under long eyelashes. Safe from the array of emotions darting in and out of her less than steady gaze.

CHAPTER TWO

'HERE, PUT THESE ON.' Alesha's dark-blond, good-looking saviour handed her one of the bags swinging from his large hand.

'Thanks,' she muttered. How embarrassing to be stuck out on the street pulling on a complete stranger's clothes. Lots better than dropping the towel though. His eyes had popped right out of his head, embarrassing her. Had he thought she'd done it on purpose? If so he must think her a bit loose. He wouldn't know that according to Luke she was the dead opposite. If only she'd been thinking straight when she went outside the apartment without keys after Karolina had specifically told her to keep them with her at all times. But she wouldn't have got an eyeful of Mr Handsome. Cherry would probably say he was fling material, but she wasn't going there. It was too soon.

Shoving her arms into the lightweight jersey, Alesha pulled it over her head, down to just above her knees. And she'd thought she was tall. The sleeves needed rolling up, but at least she felt warm and cosy. The fabric smelled of man: good-looking, intriguing man. Yes, well, she wasn't interested. As for the jeans, they were ridiculous. Even with the lengthy belt on its tightest notch they were going to slide down whenever she moved. 'Just as well I'm not going anywhere,' she quipped as she bent down to roll up the hems several turns.

'Sorry I didn't bring some shoes.'

His smile touched her deeply, dodging the lump that was Luke's defection. A genuine, not wanting anything from her smile that went some way to warming the chill gnawing at her. When was the last time a man had smiled at her like that? Had anyone ever? Finding a smile of her own, Alesha glanced down at his enormous feet. 'I doubt you have a pair of size seven high heels stashed in your wardrobe.'

His laugh was light and added to the warmth his jersey was creating. Soon she'd be roasting. 'I've never been into cross-dressing.'

'Again, thank you for everything. I don't know what I'd have done if you hadn't come along.'

'You'd have got a little colder before Karolina came to do her night round.' Kristof dug into another bag and retrieved two beers. 'I promised you one of these.'

Accepting the bottle, Alesha dug deep not to react outwardly to the zip of heat the touch of his fingers on hers created. 'What do you mean? Night round?'

His eyes had flared at that touch. Was he feeling hot too? 'Karolina checks on the apartments every morning and night, and a couple of times in between, often cleaning the pool, pulling the rare weed that dares to pop up in the gardens, making sure everyone staying here is happy. She's very particular about her apartments and wants her guests to get the most out of their time with her.'

The admiration in his voice had Alesha wondering if there was more to his relationship with this woman than he was letting on. 'The place is immaculate, and she was so welcoming that I feel terrible causing trouble. She told me to put her number in my phone, but it never crossed my mind I'd need to have it with me while I was only a few metres from my room taking a dip.' Or falling asleep. What was done was done, and there was no point bemoaning the fact she'd stuffed up.

'Karolina'll be fine. Bet it's not the first time it's happened.' Kristof broke a short bread stick in half and handed a piece over, then placed a small wedge of cheese on top of his bag along with a knife. 'Here's some nourishment. I hope you like it.'

'I'd like over-boiled cabbage at the moment.' Her gnawing stomach was doing somersaults. 'When you said you help your mother out were you referring to your medical skills?'

'I'm a general surgeon and she runs a shelter and home for children who haven't got anywhere to go, or anyone to look after them. There's a small hospital annexe attached for treating those children and others who don't make it to the main hospital. I come over for a few weeks throughout the year. I'm needed less for my surgical skills and more for general medicine, though we do some simple surgeries.'

'So it's back to basics for you when you're here.' Interesting. His mother must be important to him. Or was it those children that drew him?

'It reminds me of how I can help people in dire circumstances.' He didn't sound too happy about that. 'I also cajole colleagues in London to donate some time to help out whenever possible.' His lips pursed around the rim of his bottle. Unfortunately when he tipped his head back his Adam's apple became very prominent, and sent her stomach into squeeze-release mode, adding heat to her system, which had to be good considering how cold she'd got standing out here.

Looking away, Alesha gulped at her bottle, focusing on what his problem was, not on *him*. Didn't he like working alongside his mother? But if he got involved with organising other medical people to come across to take a turn helping then he must care about what went on in the shelter. 'You didn't mention the mental trauma some of those children must suffer. Who takes care of that?'

'My mother is a psychologist who first trained as a nurse. She also employs counsellors and other medical staff. Her hours are endless because she's driven to helping every kid that turns up on her doorstep.' Kristof's pride was tangible, but there was a chill behind it. As if he didn't approve, which wasn't making sense. 'Sometimes I wish she'd take a break, look out for herself, but it's never going to happen so I've learned to keep quiet.'

'You assist her at the home. She must be pleased about that, working with her son.'

The pride slipped. 'Yes, she is.' This time the words were clipped and there was a definite 'don't go there' warning hanging between them.

Who was she to upset the man who'd had

his plans for the evening disrupted because she'd been careless? 'London's amazing. I've been living and working there for nearly two years and I still haven't had enough.' Though she was starting to think the men in London mightn't be good for her if the way they dumped her was an indication. Another gulp of beer went down her throat. She'd survive. She always did. She was about looking after herself, had never been needy, and wasn't about to start. She took another gulp. At least the beer was refreshing.

'Where are you from? I'm picking Australia or New Zealand.'

'Kiwi through and through.' And before he thought to ask questions Alesha had no intention of answering, she went with, 'I came over on my OE after I finished training as a nurse. Living in England and visiting lots of places in Europe is what many of us like to do before settling down.' Of course, settling down meant finding someone who'd love her regardless.

'Why are you here on your own, staying at an apartment? Most single people come with a crowd of friends to stay at a cheap hotel, do the sightseeing, hit the bars and nightclubs like there's no tomorrow.'

'Now there's a thought.' The bottle was empty. Where was Karolina when an open bottle of champagne was cooling in the fridge? Food. She needed to eat, despite having already devoured her share of what Kristof had brought. The bread was soft and delicious, and the cheese to die for. The dairy companies back home didn't make cheese like this.

'You really are alone?' Disbelief echoed between them.

'What of it?' she growled. 'Not everyone has to be with someone.'

'Hey.' Kristof put his hand up. 'If I've offended you, then my apologies. Just making conversation.' He paused and a teasing smile appeared. 'I have learned you don't like carrying keys and a phone when you go out to the pool.' Did he have to sound so sexy when she wasn't interested?

'I was angry.' She was still angry. 'This is supposed to be the perfect holiday for me and my partner in a gorgeous location.' Bile rose, bitter and ghastly. Jumping up, she stomped to the roadside and peered through the gloom in both directions looking for Karolina.

'He's been held up?' came the logical question.

Spinning around, Alesha lost balance. It took some quick steps to stay upright. 'He's had a better offer.' Sex, kisses, laughter, fun. All of which he could've had with her.

'That's the pits.'

Give the man credit. He hadn't spewed sympathy when he knew nothing of the circumstances. 'It sucks.' She huffed out the air stalled in her lungs. 'I'll look on the bright side. I'm here and there's a whole town to explore out there.' She waved her hand in the general direction of the harbour, knowing full well a lot more of the city was behind the hill she was on.

'This is your first visit to Dubrovnik? I hope you have a wonderful time despite your setback. There's so much to see and do if you put your mind to it.'

A setback? Kristof didn't have a clue, or had the heart of a cold fish. But he'd already proven that particular organ was at least warm by going out of his way to help her. 'I'm sure I'll manage,' she snapped just as a car pulled into the parking bay beside them. The woman getting out of the car was Karolina. Phew. She shot across to her. 'I'm so sorry for being a nuisance. I fell asleep by the pool and the wind came up, blew my door shut.'

'It's okay. Now you'll be careful to take your keys and phone everywhere, eh?' At least her smile was friendly, as was the arm she threw around Alesha's shoulder. 'I'm glad Kristof found you.'

Ignoring how her burned skin stung under that arm, she smiled at Kristof. 'He couldn't avoid me when I attacked him in the street like a woman possessed.'

Kristof gathered up his bags. 'I think you're prone to exaggeration.' He turned to Karolina with a cute smile. 'Alesha was only slightly crazy when she charged at me demanding that I speak English and get her out of her predicament.'

'Who exaggerates?' Alesha spluttered.

'Let's go inside and retrieve those keys,' Karolina said. Then to Kristof, 'You found anyone to go with you tomorrow night?'

'No,' he growled.

'Have you been asking around? I'm sure there are plenty of girls who'd love nothing better than to go to a formal dinner with *you.*'

'Leave it, Karolina.'

Alesha grimaced. If anyone spoke to her so sharply she'd be heading for the hills. The gate was now unlocked so she slipped free to charge up the stairs. She couldn't get to her apartment and a hot shower quick enough. Too quickly. She missed seeing the final step and tripped, sprawling on the concrete, bruising her elbows and knees.

'Careful.' Strong, masculine hands reached for her, took her hands to tug her to her feet, giving her the odd sensation of being cared about. 'You really are having a bad day.'

He could've pointed out it was her own fault, that running up unfamiliar steps in clothes many sizes too big was right up there with leaping off the tenth floor of a hotel in the hope she'd make the swimming pool beneath. 'Yes, I am, and this one's on me.' She tried to pull free but Kristof held her elbow as he led her to the apartment Karolina was unlocking. Her head spun so she stopped, remained still, waiting for it to get back to normal.

'Are you all right?'

'I'm good.'

'When did you last eat a proper meal? I saw the way you hoed into that bread and cheese.'

'I had a sandwich while waiting for my flight first thing this morning.'

His sigh was full of exasperation. 'You've got to look after yourself.'

'There you go.' Karolina stepped back from unlocking the door to Alesha's apartment. 'Anything else I can do?'

Glad of the interruption from that annoying look on Kristof's face, Alesha gave Karolina the biggest smile she could dredge up. 'Nothing. I'm truly sorry about this. From now on I'm not even having a shower without my phone in the bathroom so I can call you if needed.'

Karolina slapped her forehead. 'I'd say that was a good idea but—'

'But the idea of hauling me out of the shower isn't.' This time her smile was genuine. 'I get it.' Then she had a brainwave. Going inside, she opened the fridge and grabbed the champagne. 'Would you both like a glass? My way of saying thanks.' Opening the small cupboard above the fridge, she reached for glasses, finding only one. Of course. There was one out on the decking. She'd have hers in a mug if necessary.

'Not for me. I have to be somewhere.' Karolina was already beating a fast retreat, adding to Alesha's guilt about messing up her evening. 'I'll see you tomorrow probably.' She hesitated. 'Add Kristof's number to your phone as well just in case.'

'Just in case what?' Alesha asked Karolina's retreating back.

'In case I'm unavailable,' she called over her shoulder before disappearing around the corner.

'What did I say?' The cork popped with that delightful sound that meant delicious wine. At least she'd pushed it back in tight. One thing in her favour.

'Nothing wrong. She's a busy lady.' Kristof took the bottle from her unsteady fingers. 'Let me.' He filled the glass she'd found and handed it back to her.

'You're not joining me?' A jolt of disappointment rocked her when it shouldn't. Had to be because she was feeling so down.

'I haven't finished my beer, and I've got another bottle in the bag.'

Okay, she'd go with that. But her tongue got away from her. After all, she was exhausted. 'You prefer beer to this?' She held her glass up after taking a long sip.

'Different drinks for different occasions. I was hot and frazzled walking home, and looking forward to a cold one.'

'What are you frazzled about now?' Her tongue had loosened up over the last few minutes. The tiredness was taking over, making her body ache and her head light. She should really say goodbye to Kristof and take that shower she was hanging out for before climbing into bed and catching up on sleep.

Kristof downed the rest of the beer in the first bottle and placed it in the bin under the sink. 'I'm going to get you something more than bread and cheese for dinner. Why don't you have a shower while I'm out, get into clothes that fit?'

That made sense. She had to change, give his gear back. 'Good idea. I'll get you some money for my food.'

'That won't be necessary. Anything you don't like?'

Alesha didn't expect strangers to shout her dinner. But were they still strangers? She was wearing Kristof's clothes, had drunk his beer, and he was here in her apartment. 'I eat most things.' Now he'd buy something she couldn't stand. 'I hope.' The champagne was going down nicely, untying some of the knots in her stomach. Not a bad medicine. Especially now that it was chilled to perfection.

'Relax. I won't buy anything unusual.' He was already at the door. 'I'll be about half an hour.'

'How are you going to get into the complex?'

When his eyes widened his eyebrows almost disappeared under the thick dark-blond waves lying on his forehead. 'What's your number?'

She rattled it off. First night in Dubrovnik and she was already giving out her details. She spluttered into her wine. Not bad at all for an uptight, *I don't do overly friendly* woman. Then, 'Take my keys. If you're a friend of Karolina's I'm sure I'll be safe.'

His eyebrows disappeared completely this time. But he did take the keys.

When the door closed behind Kristof she took her glass and headed for the small bathroom off to the side. One look in the mirror had her gaping. Red cheeks, sunken eyes, hair that looked as if she'd been dragged through a gorse bush backwards, and skin on her neck and shoulders the colour of strawberries. Very pretty. Her skin matched the bikini, which was something positive, she supposed.

Taking a deep drink of her champagne, she stripped away Kristof's jersey and jeans, then folded them to put in a bag for him to take home. Bringing her, a stranger, clothes had been kind. But kindness might be his middle name. He hadn't hesitated to help her out when he was apparently in a hurry to get home.

And changed circumstances or not, she shouldn't be hesitating over getting on with her holiday despite everything, should instead turn it into an opportunity. She had to stop overthinking the hurt going on in her heart.

But was the hurt *really* in her heart? Or was it her pride smarting because once again she'd got it wrong? She hadn't been good enough for a guy she'd been halfway to being in love with? Her shoulders drooped. She was trying too hard to find someone to love her unequivocally.

A sip of champagne didn't bring any answers, only the reminder that she needed to be busy and make the most of what she *did* have. Starting with another mouthful of champagne and then washing her hair. Those bruises from tripping over that step were already colouring up. Serve her right for not watching where she was going. What a day. Suddenly Alesha was ravenous. Hopefully her saviour wouldn't be too long with the food. Another glimpse of him wouldn't go astray either. So much for being unhappy about Luke.

Kristof stared at the shapely butt in front of him as Alesha reached up into the cupboard for plates. His jeans and jersey had been covering a figure that had his blood thickening and his manhood tightening. Now wearing fitted white jeans with a sleeveless turquoise top and thin-strapped sandals, Alesha looked stunning. Beyond beautiful. There were curves in all the right places, making his mouth water. But he already knew what those curves looked like, had felt their power on his libido. He could imagine those long legs wrapped around him when he should not be imagining anything of the sort. They didn't know each other. How long did it take to be attracted to a woman? Especially one as beautiful as Alesha?

She's a Kiwi; we're from different hemispheres. It wouldn't work even if I tried.

Mixed relationships, as in each partner being from a different country, did not work. Hadn't for his parents, or for him and his German wife.

'What did you get?' the woman causing his body all sorts of problems turned to ask.

'Deep fried squid and salad.'

'Yum. Exactly what I need.'

'Glad to oblige.' He looked away to gather his equilibrium around his overheated body. He did not want Alesha noticing his reaction to her. She wouldn't thank him. In the circumstances, she might find it disrespectful, if not down and out lecherous. He didn't do lecherous, thought it despicable. Women should be respected. Make that *most* women. Not his ex-wife, who had emptied his bank account and ramped up his credit cards to max while he was lying in a hospital bed recovering from surgery to fix a broken collarbone, damaged while saving *her* dratted dog from the ledge it had fallen over.

'I put your beer in the fridge while you were gone.'

Back to practical things. Food and beer. Excellent. Not sex. Excellent. *Breathe.* 'The fish restaurant was the closest and I know they do fabulous meals, having eaten there often.'

'Would you prefer a glass of champagne now?' Alesha asked. Her glass sat on the bench nearly empty.

'I'll take a pass, thanks. Shall we eat outside? There's a table under cover around the corner, and the wind's dropped. I like getting out in the fresh air after a day at work.' He didn't like the idea of being cooped up in this small inside space with Alesha. Not now he'd begun noticing more things about her best avoided. As lovely as she was, a short fling was probably not a wise move. There again, why not? Because she'd very recently been dumped. That was why. She was hurting, didn't need a rebound affair.

'Outside's good. I'm warm after my shower.' There was a slight slur going on in her speech.

He set plates and forks on either side of the table and opened the container from the restaurant. 'After you,' he said, indicating the chair opposite.

When she pulled up a chair next to the one he was going to use his first instinct was to move to the other side, but she'd be affronted and he didn't want that. After the day he'd had and spending the last hour sorting out Alesha's problem, he craved peace and quiet to eat and then he'd go back to his mother's house, hopefully for an uninterrupted night's sleep. Although that wasn't guaranteed—no one ever knew when the next child would arrive on the doorstep, brought in by the police or a distraught neighbour.

It was draining enough doing this work for a week at a time. How his mother coped year in, year out, he had no idea, except she was resilient and had come through a lot in her life, including putting up with his father's affairs to be there for her son until she finally couldn't take any more. He had nothing to complain about really and next week he'd be back in London working every hour available dealing with his scheduled list of patients that was endless.

'You've gone quiet,' Alesha commented as she loaded her plate with salad. Her shoulder bumped against his. Deliberate or accidental?

'Just letting go of the day.' He shifted his chair sideways.

'Tell me more about this place you're helping out at. It must be quite big to have an operating theatre.'

'Like I said, it's a shelter for neglected children. The operating theatre's tiny. Not a lot of operations are done there. Take today. A wee girl was found hidden in bushes under the

Dubrovnik bridge, cold, hungry and with numerous injuries. She hasn't spoken a word, has had surgery, and faced strangers poking at her and asking questions, and just stands there staring around as though nothing's real.'

'Except the pain in her heart.'

'Exactly. One look in her eyes and you can see it, you know? It's huge, and everyone accepts it's going to take a long, long time to lighten it.'

'If they ever do.' A layer of sadness settled in Alesha's eyes and voice.

She really got it. Did that mean she'd been hurt badly in the past? Or was there a massive heart inside that chest that understood people? 'At least she's safe now, but what the future holds is anyone's guess.' Kristof needed air, space. That sadness was tugging at him when it shouldn't. Standing up, he walked to the other end of the deck to stare down at the harbour filled with cruise ships. Tourists flooded Dubrovnik during the day, turning the Old City situated behind these hills into a place most locals avoided until winter, when they got the city back to themselves. At night many of the tourists would be back on board their ship making the most of the entertainment put on free of charge.

He heard a movement beside him and Alesha was standing there, her hands on the concrete wall, leaning forward to peer in the same direction as him. 'It's stunning.' So she'd joined him but wasn't continuing the conversation that had him fidgeting to get away.

He usually managed to keep the kids he saw in his mother's clinic at a distance. But today Capeka had got to him. His shield had slipped. He didn't know why, but did know it wasn't a good look. And that it couldn't happen again. Not if he intended to maintain his barriers against being in a loving relationship. 'Yes, it's magic.'

'Very different from London.'

If she was digging for information about his life back there she would need a bulldozer. He commented, 'We don't get the wonderful weather, for starters.'

Her mouth flattened. Then turned up into a grin. 'Fair enough.' The grin was quickly followed by a yawn. 'Sorry. It's been quite a day on top of a long night. I didn't knock off work until eleven last night and since it was my last time on the ward there was a visit to the pub involved afterwards. Then today Luke's bombshell really sank in when I stepped out of the plane into Croatia.'

'I'll leave you alone, then.' Kristof's jaw dropped. He didn't want to go. He really didn't, instead wanted to hold her close, kiss away that hurt that had started going on in her eyes when she'd mentioned a big day. 'Are you going to be all right?'

Wipe your mouth out. You don't do personal questions. With anyone.

It brought people close when he learned what made them tick, meant he could no longer put them in a box.

Alesha blinked, hard. Her mouth flattened. He didn't like that. Nor that slumping that sloped her shoulders.

'Sorry, don't answer that. It's none of my business.' But if he could make her feel a bit happier, he would.

'We planned this trip at Easter. Then a couple of weeks ago I learned I was the only one flying to Dubrovnik. Luke has found someone else and they've gone to Paris for the weekend.'

That was appalling. Who did that? 'Can I swear?'

'Go ahead but it won't change anything.' She'd crossed her arms and those long manicured fingernails were digging into her biceps.

He'd prefer they were on his biceps. Kristof stepped closer so his arm touched hers. That was as close as he was getting, tantalising fingers or not. But hell, he wanted to pull her into his arms and kiss that sadness away. Even when the man she'd want kissing her wasn't him.

Alesha leaned into him, as though now she'd voiced what had happened the strength to stay upright had deserted her.

He couldn't resist. His arm wound around her shoulders, to give her support. Nothing more. Or was it? A heady mix of gentleness, need and friendship closed around him. A totally foreign sensation. He lost track of how long they stood there, both staring out across the harbour with a myriad lights winking from the ships and the wharves, he holding her, she trembling.

Then she knocked him sideways with a whisper. 'You don't have to go. I could do with some company.' When she turned to face him she was close so her breasts brushed against his chest. When her mouth touched his, those lips were soft and warm, exciting, just as he'd imagined. Talk about getting what he wished for.

Kristof lifted his chin and stepped back, his hands on her shoulders until she found her balance. 'Thank you for asking but you're feeling let down, unhappy, disappointed. Tomorrow you'll regret having made that suggestion.' He was already regretting not following through. As far as kisses went that one had barely got started, but every cell in his body was screaming out for more and for the follow-up rampant sex.

'That's a no, then.'

'Yes, Alesha, it is.' Give him strength, because the more he said no, the more he knew it was a lie, that he wanted to accept her invitation, to lose himself in her, give her a reason to let go the hurt plaguing her eyes for a few hours at least.

'I could beg.' Fixed on him, her eyes were enormous.

'It wouldn't become you.' His lips grazed her forehead. He breathed in apples from her hair.

Go, while you still can.

Dropping his hands, he stepped further away. 'Take care, Alesha. Whatever you do, enjoy your time in Croatia.' And on that dry note he left, feeling her eyes boring into his back until he reached the bottom step and let himself out onto the street. He didn't know if she watched from above as he walked up the road, wasn't looking back over his shoulder to find out. Alesha had come into his life with a problem. Now the crisis was fixed and with every step he took he was leaving her further behind, safe, out of his life, out of the way of temptation. He couldn't fix her bigger problem.

'Kristof, wait. Stop. Look up the road.' Alesha was running after him. 'I think there's a fire further up.' She had his arm now, was pulling at him and pointing towards the area where his mother's house was.

A red glow backlit a building. Not his mother's, but close. Someone's house was definitely burning. 'I'm calling the emergency services. You go back inside.' He didn't need to be worrying about Alesha while he tried to assess the situation.

'I'm coming with you. There could be people inside.'

Arguing wasted time. 'What can you do to help?' It was an honest question. If she was hanging around there might be something she could do to help.

'I'm a nurse, remember?'

'Come on.' There wasn't time to argue, and she was right, she might be needed. He began sprinting up the road. Hopefully she wasn't going to be required at the scene of the fire.

Puff, puff, from beside him. Not a fit nurse, then.

The emergency dispatch for the city answered his call, preventing him saying something he'd regret. Rattling off what he knew about the location, nothing specific but once the emergency crews got close they'd work it out, he punched the red icon and shoved the phone deep into his pocket, hoping it stayed there while he got on with helping out at the fire. Losing all his work contacts was not on.

You don't want to lose Alesha's number either.

Best if he did, then he couldn't be tempted into calling her, asking her to join him for a beer or a trip into town for a meal during the coming week.

Kristof really was trying to fool himself. Who needed a number when he walked by the apartment complex every day? Which reminded him. 'Did you remember your keys?'

She gaped at him, her eyes wide and filled with disgust. 'Guess it really isn't my day.'

They weren't going to call Karolina out a second time. 'There's a spare bed at my mother's.'

Laughter filled the now smoky air. 'I meant there went my opportunity to crash at your place. I have keys and phone buttoned into my back pocket.'

He looked. How could he not? Yes, there,

on that smooth, curved outline of her back-side, was the obvious shape of a phone and a bundle of keys. 'Well done.'

Damn.

CHAPTER THREE

ALESHA DREW DEEP breaths in an attempt to stop puffing so hard. Time to find a gym if this was what a short run up a gently sloping hill did. Beside her Kristof was barely breathing any faster than normal.

'Bystanders are saying there's a family of four inside,' he told her. 'I'm going to see how close I can get.'

'Be careful.' Look out for yourself, don't get injured. Clench, clench went her stomach for her new— What? Friend?

She couldn't hear any sirens. 'How far away is the fire station?' She picked her way through the crowd behind him.

'Ten minutes. Stay back here.'

'And if you find someone in need of medical attention?'

'We'll bring them out here and you can help me.'

'We?' That was when she realised two other

men were pushing ahead on the same track Kristof was following. 'Fine.' She was wasting precious time, holding him back from possibly saving someone. 'Go.' Her heart sank. If there really was a family in that inferno their chances of survival were slim, and getting smaller by the second. When she was training back in Christchurch she'd worked in a burns unit and had hated it. The stench, the raw agony, the horror in her patients' eyes as they stared at their scars, had drained her emotionally in a way no other field of nursing had.

Around her people were talking as they gaped at the scene. Unfortunately she couldn't understand a word. Someone pointed towards the house and there was a shout as a burning piece from the roof plunged to the ground. Kristof towered above everyone, making it easy to keep an eye on his progress.

Be safe, please.

He was in charge. No doubt about that. He seemed the kind of guy who'd take note of the situation and still charge in to save whoever he could with little regard for his own safety. Not that she could explain why she felt that, she just did. He'd impressed her with the way he'd looked after her earlier. No one had ever gone out of their way for her before, and it made her feel special, as if she counted for something. Then she'd repaid him by coming on to him. It was a wonder he'd spoken to her at all after that.

'Does anyone know if the family was definitely at home when the fire broke out?' she asked without thinking, and got a surprise.

'The mother and son came home thirty minutes ago,' the woman beside her answered. 'The husband and other son are still out.'

'Two safe. That's a start.' Where had Kristof gone? There was no way he could get inside. Not and survive. It was a furnace in there.

'I hear sirens,' said the woman.

There was movement ahead, and the crowd parted. Kristof strode towards her, a body in his arms. 'Alesha? I've got the lad. He's unconscious.' Kneeling down, he laid his precious bundle on the ground.

Running forward, she dropped to her knees, ignored the gravel digging into the earlier bruises. 'That's a nasty cut on his head.' Blood oozed through the lad's hair. Her fingers gently probed, touched swollen flesh. 'Something must've fallen on him. Where did you find him? You'd better not have gone inside.' What did that matter now? If he had he was out safe.

'On the back porch lying half out the door.' Kristof began checking the boy over, gently rolling him onto his right side. 'Burns to his back and left arm.'

'Don't pull that shirt off,' she warned. They didn't need to cause any further damage.

'Agreed.' Kristof was feeling the bones in an oddly shaped elbow, a competent doctor at work. 'Fractures for sure. He's got cuts as well as massive trauma bruising. Someone mentioned an explosion.'

'Do people here use gas for cooking?' That could explain the injuries and the fire.

'Yes.' He gave her a nod of acknowledgment. 'You know your stuff.'

'Worked in a burns unit. He has respiratory problems, probably due to smoke inhalation.'

'I'll check his heart.'

Cardiac arrest often followed respiratory failure. 'Will an ambulance come with that fire engine?' A defibrillator wouldn't go astray right now, just in case of the worst-case scenario.

'Of course. From what I'm hearing two fire trucks and one ambulance have just pulled up. The good news is the hospital is only a mile further up the road.'

'Knowing the lingo is a plus.' Never had she felt so useless. Not understanding what was going on was disturbing. But she did understand this boy's dilemma and that was all that really mattered. He needed her help, not her doubts and frustration.

'Great nursing skills don't need interpreting.' Kristof underscored her thoughts as his hand touched the back of hers briefly. Except she hadn't thought *great* was true, just thorough.

Someone in uniform knelt beside her, asking rapid questions in Croatian. No doubt a paramedic. She locked eyes on Kristof. 'You take this.'

He was already talking to the other man. She continued taking the boy's pulse for a second time. 'Slower.'

Another person in ambulance uniform joined them and Alesha was nudged aside. Her back cricked as she stood up and looked around. 'What about the mother?'

Screams rent the air. Someone was pushing through the crowd. A woman. In her late thirties? The boy's mother? Alesha crossed her fingers. That would mean she was safe and not inside. The woman dropped to the ground beside the boy, crying and shouting, reaching to touch her son, being gently held back by Kristof and another lady.

Alesha stepped away. The woman's grief was personal, and heart-wrenching. On the other side of the road she stopped amidst the crowd to take stock. Around her voices were low and all eyes seemed to be on the mother and boy. Time to head back to the apartment. There was nothing else she could do to help here.

'He's going to be in hospital for a while but I think he'll be all right.' Kristof materialised out of the gloom. 'None of those injuries look life-threatening.'

'If you don't count the scars he'll have.'

'True.' His sigh echoed her own. 'I'll see you back to the apartment.'

'That's not necessary. It's only a few hundred metres down the road.'

'I don't care if it's next door. I'm coming with you.'

Nice. Especially when she'd all but thrown herself at him. 'Thanks.' Maybe this time she'd finally get to bed to catch up on some sleep. Alone, and right now that didn't seem as lonely as it should. It was a normal state.

A sound like a sweeping broom from outside her room penetrated Alesha's mind, bringing her to the surface of the sleep that had dragged her under the moment she'd dropped onto the bed after getting back from the fire. Judging by the smell of smoke, she should've showered but falling asleep under the water jet wouldn't have been a bright idea. Her shirt was rucked up to her breasts but it seemed she had managed to pull her jeans off.

The good news was she'd slept all night. Picking up her phone from the floor, she gasped. It was nearly one in the afternoon. Half the day had gone. What a waste when Dubrovnik was out there, waiting to be investigated.

Swinging her legs over the bed, she sat up and instantly dropped her pounding head into her hands. Too much sleep did that. And too many glasses of champagne on an empty stomach. The half-full bottle mocked her from the bench. Another waste, but thank goodness she hadn't drunk it all or she wouldn't have been able to help with that boy last night. Nor would she be feeling semi good to go today. What had she been thinking to have beer and champagne? It was so not her, but nothing about last night had been. On the other hand, last time she got dumped she might have packed a sad and had a few drinks, but she hadn't locked herself out in a foreign country or made a pass at a relative stranger. Throw in the fire and it'd been a drama-filled night.

How was that boy today? Hopefully he'd be heavily sedated to allow those burns time to settle down. Days, if not weeks, of painkillers and heavy doses of antibiotics were ahead for him.

Picking up her jeans, she grimaced at the not so white fabric. Dirt from kneeling on the ground by the boy looked as if it would never come out, but she'd throw them in the laundry in case she got lucky.

Heading for the shower, she tripped over a bag. Kristof's clothes. He'd forgotten them in his hurry to get away from her. Now what? Could she nail them to the wall outside the gate for when he walked home tonight?

Swish, swish. The sound that had woken her. Opening the wooden blinds showed Karolina sweeping the deck that covered the width of the property and right back to the table where she'd eaten squid with Kristof. Karolina would know where to find the children's home. It wouldn't be a problem to drop the bag off there on her way to the Old City. She also owed Kristof an apology for her untoward behaviour while they were eating. What had possessed her? Apart from feeling unloved and a teeny bit in awe of him?

With a towel wrapped around her waist, she snatched up her keys and headed outside. 'Karolina, hi.'

The woman turned, her long, thick ponytail flicking across her back. 'I hear we have you to thank for young Stevan surviving the blaze that destroyed his family's home. You and Kristof.'

'There were other people there more qualified to look after him. How is Stevan today?' Knowing his name brought him closer.

'He's in—how do you say—Intensive Care?' Alesha nodded. 'That's it.'

'Heavily sedated?'

Again, Alesha nodded.

'For the pain from the burns and the operation on his shoulder, or was it his arm? I'm not certain.'

'Probably shoulder from what I saw. He's going to be in hospital for a while.' Alesha drew a breath. 'Karolina, can you tell me where the children's home is? I've got a bag to drop off there.'

'It's easy. Come and I show you how to get there.' She headed for the wall that overlooked the street below and the harbour beyond. 'See that building at the bottom of the hill behind those shops? That's it. I will draw on your street map how to get there. It's not far, fifteen minutes' walking.'

'If I don't get lost.' Alesha laughed, ignoring the thrill of excitement in her veins. Here was a foreign town and she was about to go exploring. Travel was her favourite pastime when she wasn't nursing. At last she was behaving sensibly, accepting her lot and not getting in a pickle about it. 'Though getting lost can be fun in strange cities, as long as I find my way out again without getting into seedy places.'

'You'll be good down there, nowhere nasty. But with the map it is easy. Then where are you going after the refuge?'

'To the Old City to have a look around, maybe take a tour up to the lookout.' The tour took only a couple of hours and there was still plenty of time left today. If she hurried. 'I'd better get showered and dressed. I only just woke up.'

'It was an eventful night for you.' Karolina chuckled as if it was a huge joke.

'It sure was. And now I've wasted enough of the day as it is.' She turned for her apartment only to have Karolina follow.

'I'll mark the map for you. Have you had breakfast?'

'No. I'll get something on the way to the shelter. But a coffee wouldn't go astray.' She filled the kettle and plugged it in while Karolina found the map on the shelf where the city info brochures lay.

'There're two good bakeries on the road below this one.' She marked the map with two crosses. 'Here is Kristof's mother's place where the children stay.' She drew a big X over the spot with a circle around it.

'That's great. Thanks. Do you want a coffee?' Now why offer that when she was suddenly in a hurry to get moving? Because she liked this woman who hadn't gone ape at her for forgetting her keys last night, and was more than helpful today. Because this holiday alone wasn't how it was meant to be and she wouldn't mind a bit of company.

'A quick one. I have to be at work in forty-five minutes. I'll make it while you get ready.'

'You have another job as well as running this place?'

'Yes, because in winter there are not many guests so I need to keep the money coming.'

'Mortgages don't pay themselves, eh?' No wonder there were shadows beneath Karolina's eyes. 'I'll be fast. Milk, no sugar, please.'

After rubbing sunscreen on every bit of skin that might be seen by the sun and slapping her make-up on with less care than normal Alesha dressed in navy shorts and a snappy white shirt with thin darts down the front to accentuate her shape. There no hiding her height so she always aimed to draw attention to her breasts and hips.

'Out here,' Karolina called when she left the bathroom. 'On the deck under the umbrella.'

Where she and Kristof had sat last night. Only he'd taken up a lot more space with his long legs and large, muscular frame. Hard to imagine someone so big doing delicate surgical procedures, but she'd seen it before when she worked in Theatre, and knew men could be as careful and light with their sewing skills as a woman. How gentle would Kristof's fingers be on her skin?

Gasp. Stop thinking these random thoughts.

'If you like I can walk part of the way with you. My work is in the same direction.'

'That'd be great.' Alesha gulped down her coffee. 'I know you're in a hurry. I'll just get my bag.'

'And keys.' Another laugh.

'Not likely to forget them again.' At her side she crossed her fingers for good measure.

The sun beat down as Alesha walked down the steps that led from one street to the next further down the hill. After the previous wet, cool week in London the heat was heaven, and gave her another pang of nostalgia for summer at home. She was getting quite a few of those at the moment. Not that home was warm when she factored in her family, but she was not going there today when she was in paradise.

Her destination became apparent once she

reached the harbour, a collection of low houses joined together with what must be corridors, and all tucked against the hill, bathed in sun. While it wasn't glamorous it was warm and welcoming. The front door stood wide open, and since no one was about she walked in, calling, 'Hello?' as she made her way to the desk at the end of the hallway. 'Hello?' The colours were bright: pinks, greens, blues, yellow. Done for children, not to win a prize in a homemaker magazine.

'Can I help you?' she was asked in a classy Croatian English accent.

Alesha looked back the way she'd come to see an older, tall woman coming towards her. 'Hello. I'm Alesha Milligan, a visitor to Dubrovnik.' Was this Kristof's mother? The eyes were the same mesmerising blue-grey shade. 'I'm the idiot who locked herself out of her apartment.'

'Now I know who you are.' The woman's face relaxed, her smile wide and friendly. 'You're the nurse who helped the boy caught up in the fire last night.' When Alesha raised an eyebrow at her, she added, 'My son mentioned you this morning.'

'He did?' There was a surprise. She'd have thought Kristof would have put her to the back of his mind the moment he'd seen her through the gate for the second time. 'I suppose every-one's talking about the fire. It was awful.'

'It could've been worse.' In the lady's face there was sympathy along with a load of ac-ceptance for what life threw at people. 'The consequences of not using a gas tank properly.'

Had that been established already? Alesha wasn't getting into details. She didn't intend hanging around long enough to become in-volved in local events, other than what had happened last night. She shifted her balance, held up the bag of clothes. 'I'm returning Kristof's things. I probably shouldn't have come here but I don't know where he stays.'

I'd like to touch base with him, apologise again for being too forward.

'You are most welcome here. Unfortunately, my son's in Theatre at the moment. Remov-ing an appendix for a young girl. It gives her merry hell regularly, but isn't serious enough for the hospital to fix so he's doing it. It's our second appendectomy in two days.'

'Her family must be relieved you can help.' It was a shame she wouldn't be seeing Kristof. He'd been her saviour. 'Can you tell Kristof I said thanks, um, and sorry, please?'

'Sorry?'

Trust this woman to pick up on that. As as-tute as her son. 'I wasn't in a good frame of mind last night. Before we attended the fire,' Alesha hastened to add, not wanting anyone to think she'd done something wrong by attending the boy.

'Kristof won't be long. Would you like to look around our establishment while you wait?' The woman was already walking towards a door, as though Alesha was expected to follow.

'I'm on my way to the Old City to take a mini tour up the hill and to some tiny waterfall near the border.'

'It'll still be there tomorrow.' Mrs Montfort glanced over her shoulder. 'I'd really like to show you what we are doing here.'

Why? 'I'm only in town for a few days.'

'So Kristof tells me.' She held a door open. 'By the way, I'm Antonija.'

Certain she was being played, but with no idea what for, Alesha gave in and followed, partly because she hated saying no, and partly because her interest had been piqued last night when Kristof talked briefly about his work here. 'Tell me how the place operates. Do some of the children stay long term?'

'We have permanent children, though we're always trying to find families to adopt those. Then there are others who are brought in by strangers or the police who've been abused, abandoned, or have run away from who knows what.' The older woman's voice darkened. 'Some go home again, or to relatives; some into state care, and others become our temporary residents.'

'That's so unfair. How do you cope with this day in, day out?' Alesha's heart was breaking and she hadn't met any of the children.

'With dignity, love, and difficulty.'

Talk about honest. How many people would admit to a stranger that it was tough doing what she did? Alesha smiled. 'You must be a very special lady.'

The smile she got back was soft. 'Thank you, dear. I'm not alone. There are a lot of kind people out there, some of whom come here to help.' Then she turned brisk. 'Come and meet some of the children. This is the classroom.' Judging by the racket when she opened the door, the teacher was as much in charge as a sheepdog rounding up a herd of cattle. 'They might be a bit nervous but don't let that stop you being at ease with them.'

This woman didn't know her. 'I won't.'

Alesha stepped inside and smiled. There was nothing particularly unusual about the room or the children. They were all dressed in mismatched clothes, and their faces and hair shone. Most of them sat at desks with books open, books they were ignoring, until one by one they became aware of Antonija and quietened down.

Alesha bit down on the urge to laugh. Undoing Antonija's effect wasn't on if she wanted to get out of here in one piece. Because she had no doubt this woman could be fierce if needed, and when it came to disrupting the children fierce might be needed. She'd seen a similar determination to do what was right in Kristof's eyes when they approached that burning house. And when he'd backed away from her advances. Heat filled her cheeks and her arms tightened against her sides. What an idiot she'd been.

Antonija spoke to the children in Croatian before explaining to Alesha, 'I've told them your name and that you're visiting from London.'

How much had Kristof talked about her that morning? And why? He'd been all too happy to finally say goodnight when he'd returned her to the apartment so she'd thought he'd have all but forgotten her by breakfast.

The kids were all staring at her, some giggling. All except one. A skinny child—the long hair suggested a girl—stood stock-still in the far corner, one leg tucked behind the other, one hand gripped tight at her side while the other arm was encased in a sling. But worse than that, more heart-rending, was the blank expression on her face, closely followed by the incomprehension in her eyes. No one so young should ever feel that lost and confused. Except they could, and often did. And it was the most hideous place to be.

Alesha's heart heaved. She wanted to race across and bundle the child up into her arms and hold her until her eyes cleared—which would take months, if not years. She didn't move. Frightening the girl further would be the worst thing possible. That girl was putting it out there, 'don't come near'. 'The poor darling,' she whispered.

'Capeka is our latest visitor.

'Visitor?'

'For lack of a better word. I don't like calling them waifs or strays. She was found under a bridge by strangers, who brought her to us yesterday.'

Alesha nodded. 'Kristof operated on her.'

'He mentioned that? To you?' Surprise rippled off the woman. 'Sorry, that wasn't meant in an offensive way, but my son never talks about his patients. Especially not the ones he sees in here.'

'Guess he thought it didn't matter when we're not going to see each other again.'

'Really?'

Alesha had no idea what this lady was asking about. Kristof telling her about the girl? Or that she wouldn't see him again? It didn't matter, though disappointment rippled through her at the thought of not seeing him once more. Now that she was fully awake, not half naked and exhausted, nor feeling as let down as she probably should, Kristof would probably look like an everyday guy. One she'd not think about at unexpected moments. 'Does Capeka stand in the corner all the time? She doesn't join the other children?'

'Not yet. It's early days. Sometimes it takes for ever for a child who comes here to feel accepted. She's watching you, though. Interesting. Still, we'll leave her alone to make her own mind up about whether to join in or not. Come and see the rest of the centre.'

There went her sightseeing, but it didn't matter. She was more than happy to take a look around the home.

Nearly an hour later Alesha found herself wandering into the classroom again. This time she was alone, and the children were quiet, working on an exercise the teacher had set. Capeka remained in the corner, her eyes averted, and yet Alesha would swear the malnourished girl was aware of every move, every word uttered, by the children and the teacher. Nodding to the teacher, she went to sit on a chair at the back of the room, not intruding on Capeka but close enough to be there for her. Not that she had anything other than life skills to help someone with this child's problems, and that wouldn't be enough, but she wanted, needed, to be there for her. Wanted to send warm vibes across the gap between them, to let her know she wasn't alone, and was in good care now. That there were good people who'd never hurt her.

Picking up a children's book from the table beside her, she slowly turned the pages, not able to read the words, but murmuring her own version of the story. Not hard to do when the pictures suggested it might be a classic from her own childhood. When she reached the end she started again. And again. Until she felt Capeka's gaze on her. Then she read the story again. The child wouldn't have a clue if she was telling the story correctly or making up a load of nonsense but hopefully she heard the genuine empathy in her voice. As long as Capeka watched her she'd continue telling the same story over and over.

Kristof stood in the classroom doorway, flabbergasted. Alesha. What was she doing at the refuge? And in this room at that? Strange how there were nine children in here yet only one was fully aware of her.

Capeka was fixated on the woman reading a story out loud. Staring, unafraid of Alesha. Though there was no way the kid understood a word she was saying she seemed to understand the light, carefree cadence, the soothing facial expressions, the gentleness, the slow way Alesha turned the pages and touched the pictures. If little Capeka was so taken with her that for the first time since her arrival she was actively watching an adult, then he'd go get a bed for Alesha immediately. She was needed around here.

There was still caution in the girl's expression as she listened, watched, standing in that awkward position. What that was doing to her leg muscles was anyone's guess. The tension was there in tight tendons, and that clenched fist. In the pain in her eyes. But those eyes were glued to Alesha. Interesting.

'I've never seen anything like it,' his mother whispered.

He flicked her a look. 'Bottle her.' He'd forgotten his mother had been behind him, and he never forgot when she was around. Keeping his guard up was automatic since his marriage imploded back when he believed in happily ever after. Before his father finished off that belief once and for ever. Before the guilt over blaming his mother for everything that went wrong in their family landed on his shoulders. He had to admit it, Alesha had intrigued him from the get-go with those beautiful eyes and that wonderful figure. Then there was her laughter and willingness to enjoy herself despite everything.

It seemed that around Alesha Milligan he had to be doubly vigilant.

His mother said quietly, 'I'm going to ask her if she'll drop in every day to spend time doing this with Capeka until she goes home.'

'London, not home,' he countered automatically. Keeping things correct was another habit from the past.

'London? That's handy.' His mother looked up at him with a curious look in her shrewd eyes.

A look that paralysed him. Trouble was brewing and he wasn't going to like it. But forewarned gave him time to prepare—if only he knew what he was arming up for. Unless he was being precious and it wasn't him she was targeting at all, but merely getting help for Capeka from any source available. That was his mother to a tee. But the sneaking suspicion going on in the back of his head that this was about him couldn't be denied, not totally. He needed to stay prepared, ready for anything. 'Don't even bother,' he retorted just in case he was right.

She was impaling him with a smug smile. 'Fine.'

Stepping away from his mother, he carefully closed the door, effectively shutting her out, and leaned back against it. It was hard to ignore that chuckle from the other side of the door though. His eyes sought a diversion. Alesha. Without all that stress going on she was more beautiful than he remembered. Her skin was peaches and cream, English rather than the outdoorsy skin that the few New Zealand women he'd met at the hospital seemed to gain over years in the sun. The smattering of freckles on her cheeks was cute, and added to her intrigue, giving an air of innocence that the wariness in her eyes refuted. Her simple white shirt was the perfect contrast for her golden brown hair tied back loosely into a thick braid. No doubt the temperature was too high to wear it out, which was a shame. Last night her hair had been a mess, all over the show, and very compelling. It had taken strength not to run his fingers through those rampant curls.

Why did she do this to him? What was different about Alesha that fizzed his blood in a way other women didn't? Whatever, he wasn't going to waste time figuring it out. They weren't going to be a 'they'.

There was no denying the churning going on in his belly, though, while Alesha looked the epitome of calmness sitting on that uncomfortable chair making up a story for a sad little girl. Too much so for his comfort. Because he didn't believe it. There was history in her face and expressions, last night and now, that spoke of knowledge of Capeka's pain. Knowledge gained from experience. Someone had hurt her, and he didn't believe it was just that man who dumped her unceremoniously before her holiday. That had hurt her, no doubt, but there'd been more anger than the deep, gutting pain that a broken heart would cause. He should know. He'd been there.

Maybe he should've taken her up on that offer she'd made by placing her mouth on his. He was not averse to a fling with a beautiful and willing woman. There was red blood in his veins, after all. Sex without strings. Add in a meal or two, sharing a glass of champagne, and it sounded good to him. Especially when he'd be heading back home to London next Saturday.

Alesha lives in London.

London was huge. They'd never bump into each other unless it was deliberate, and why would it be? He hadn't found out where she worked, and had no intention of doing so. She might be a nurse but there were many hospitals and medical service centres around the city.

Right then the woman causing his brain fade looked up and locked startled eyes on him, crimson creeping into her cheeks. 'Hello,' she said quietly.

He crossed the room and straddled a chair, his hands on the back as he studied her. 'Hello back.'

Her gaze dropped to the book and once again she began telling a story.

A quick glance showed Capeka wearing a frown and her head lowered. He'd wrecked the moment. 'Sorry,' he said as quietly as possible. 'I should've thought before I acted.'

It's your fault for getting in my head.

'It's okay. She's tiring anyway. It wasn't as though she was about to run across and crawl onto my knee. Unfortunately, that's going to take a lot of time and care so it won't be me she finally trusts enough to get close to.'

'You're starting the process though. That's good.' Last night he'd been thinking she was a bit of a loose cannon with her stress, drinking and that kiss. Though not at the fire. There she'd been calm and efficient, skilful and caring as she helped young Stevan. Nor did that describe the quiet, contained woman sitting opposite him now. Not even close. First impressions didn't always pan out. But usually he first got suckered into believing the woman was wonderful when really she was a conniving scheme wanting something from him. Could second impressions be just as wrong? Please no. So far all Alesha had wanted from him was a kiss and maybe follow-up sex. He couldn't argue with that. It certainly didn't appear to come with the *I'm taking all you've got* attitude of his ex.

You didn't see it with her until it was too late either, he warned himself.

Sweat broke out on his brow. It was time to get out of here, go find a kid who needed his attention, because right now his brain was on the blink, focusing on Alesha when it knew better. He wasn't in the market for a woman.

Hot and Alesha were suddenly in the same thought. His fingers dragged down his face. This was absolutely bat crazy. Get out of here.

Alesha stood up, unfolding her body slowly. 'I brought your clothes back.'

'I saw a bag on my mother's desk. Thank you.' He had to turn away or drown in the deep brown speckled pools fixed on him, full of nothing but friendship. Friendship was good. Even Alesha's wary version. It wasn't enough.

Had to be more than enough. He wasn't about to add to her hurt. But he could alleviate it for a while.

'Easy. Our girl's watching you from under her eyebrows.' There was hope in Alesha's voice.

'Capeka. It means stork.'

'I heard.' Low laughter erupted from that sensuous mouth. 'It suits her. Not sure that's good, but if it works then what does it matter?'

'Capeka.' Kristof spoke softly in Croatian. 'Did you like Alesha's story?'

The girl nibbled her bottom lip and stared at the floor. Then slowly she nodded, once.

Alesha looked from the girl to him. 'What did you say?'

'She'd like you to come back and read to her again.' Sort of. What had possessed him to say that? He didn't want her hanging around here. Not when his belly knotted and his groin tightened just being in the same room. All very well to think a quick fling was a good idea, but every time he saw that darkness at the back of Alesha's gaze he knew he had to stay away. Adding to her pain was not happening on his watch.

'No problem. I'll drop in tomorrow.'

No surprise there. 'This could put restraints

on your sightseeing.' He hadn't forgotten why she was here.

'I'm sure I can fit it all in.' Alesha closed the book and placed it on the table. Nodding at Capeka, she smiled. 'I'll be back tomorrow morning.' Then she headed for the door.

Kristof translated before following. And promptly wished he hadn't when his mother confronted him.

'Kristof, you said you couldn't find anyone to take as your partner to the fundraising dinner. I'd like you to take Alesha as a thank you to her for spending time with Capeka.'

'Mother,' he growled. 'There are reasons I am going alone.' Not that he could remember what they were right now, other than he hated charity functions with a passion. Sure, they raised the money needed for the cause, but he preferred to write a cheque any day. No palavering to be had. No smiling to people who'd done their damnedest to outbid everyone else just to prove they could.

'Alesha.' His mother had turned her shoulder on him. 'Tonight there's a dinner in the Old City to raise funds for the shelter and I'd like you to join us.'

Alesha would say no. So far she didn't seem to be the type who liked all that hype either.

'Really? That would be lovely, thank you. What time and where?'

Third impression—Alesha liked to socialise, and there would be her favourite champagne on tap too. He hadn't done very well at reading her at all.

His mother turned to him. 'Kristof will pick you up at seven.'

Thank you, Mum.

Short of looking and sounding unreasonable, he was stuck with bowing to her wishes and accompanying this woman to a dinner he did not want to attend. But he owed his mother. Always had, always would.

Bring it on.

CHAPTER FOUR

KRISTOF DIDN'T WANT to take her to the dinner. Alesha sighed her disappointment. There'd been no missing the annoyance that had flared in his face when his mother had told her he'd pick her up at seven. He was so obviously uninterested in her in any way, shape or form that it was going to be a long night having to sit side by side pretending they were comfortable with each other. To think she'd thrown herself at him last night. Thank goodness one of them had been thinking straight.

She really was a slow learner. To do that only weeks after Luke had dumped her, proving once again men weren't interested in her for anything but having a good time, a short good time at that, showed she'd hit rock bottom. Maybe she hadn't loved him as in completely and utterly, but her feelings for him had been strong and, she'd believed, growing. Could it be she hadn't loved him but loved the idea he might be the one? How long was she going to carry on believing there might be a man out there who could love her for all of her? Come on. She didn't truly, deep down, believe that. No, it was hope for the impossible that got in the way. Hope that had her taking chances that always backfired. Hope that because her parents stopped loving her didn't mean someone else would.

Alesha stared at her image in the small mirror in the apartment and twisted around to check the back of her fitted red dress. Red was this season's top colour and suited her well. Even if she said so herself she didn't scrub up too badly. Eat your heart out, Luke. Her shoulders slumped. Bet he was having a barrel of fun with *the one* in Paris, and hadn't thought of her once. Why would he when she was obviously yesterday's bread?

Stop it. She was going out to a dinner and auction with a gorgeous man in a city she'd never seen before. Take the positives and forget all about what might've been. A giggle escaped. She wasn't going to understand most of what went on so she could make fun filling in the gaps.

The zip had three inches to go and she couldn't reach it. She'd go knock on another apartment door if she thought any other guests were in, but she already knew they weren't. The complex had been eerily quiet when she returned from walking along Port Cruz.

Voices outside drew her attention. Karolina and—and Kristof. Bang on seven o'clock. Downing the last of the water in her glass, she picked up her keys and phone, shoved them in her clutch purse before drawing a deep breath and stepping outside. Almost into Kristof's arms as he reached to knock on the doorframe. 'Oh, hello,' she gasped, her gaze filled with an expanse of white-shirt-covered chest.

Kristof stepped back, taking that manly scent with him. 'You look stunning.'

Lifting her head, she stared up into warm eyes that didn't seem to be filled with a hidden agenda. 'Thank you.'

Don't let that go to your head.

It wasn't the first time a man had said the same, yet when Kristof spoke in that husky, warm voice that sent shivers down her spine she wanted to believe him more than she'd believed anyone before. Silly girl. Had she already forgotten her determination to be careful, and remain aloof from now on? If only she knew how to do that then she wouldn't get hurt. She turned to close her door.

'Stand still while I pull your zip up.' It was a command, not said with amusement or longing.

How had she forgotten the zip? Because Kristof stole the capability to think, to remember, to act normally. 'Sure.' Heat tiptoed into her skin where his fingers brushed, and even where they didn't. A quick tug and she was all done up, and free of him. This was going to be a very long night. She spun around. 'Let's go.' Being unpunctual was not her.

Kristof took her hand and placed it on his arm. 'Let's.'

On the short drive to the Old City Kristof pointed out landmarks and the quickest way for her to walk from the apartment when she wanted to go on the tour she'd missed out on that day. So far so good. The tension gripping her since he'd appeared at her door backed off, making it easy to chat with him. When she wasn't trying to ignore how handsome he was, or how sexy those black trousers, white shirt and black dinner jacket made him look, that was.

'You have to make time to wander around this city, day and night. It's special,' Kristof told her as they walked hand in hand—so she didn't slip on her heels apparently—down the sloping ancient road into the centre of the city where tables had been set up under large sun umbrellas outside a restaurant.

Stopping to stare around at the buildings and

parapets, and the paved road, Alesha nodded. 'I can never get enough of these old towns. Back home old means weatherboard houses and simplistic churches. Nothing as beautiful as this.'

He laughed. 'I hear there are wonderful mountains and green hills for miles, and the sea is never far away.'

'Yes, there are those.' Another pang of homesickness knocked. Why? It wasn't as though she had family or close friends hankering for her return. But this going it alone meant being lonely at times, which was when she usually made the mistake of trying to get close to a man. Sucking her stomach in and tightening her shoulders, she got on with enjoying the evening with Kristof. 'Home is where the heart is—' though hers had gone AWOL '—and all that, but at the moment I'm having a great time discovering the northern hemisphere.'

Kristof nudged her towards the restaurant. 'So you're out to conquer the world? Or running away from home?'

Too close to the mark to acknowledge. 'Definitely conquering.'

'Let's find our seats and get a glass of your favourite tipple, then you can tell me about the places you've been.'

They were shown to the top table, and as Kristof held out her chair he was grumbling under his breath.

'Problem?' she asked.

A spark flared in his eyes as he leaned close. 'If we were seated at the back we could escape early. Now we're stuck to the bitter end.' His gaze seemed fixed on her, which didn't go with the bitter bit of his comment. That was a very heated gaze, stirring her in places that didn't need stirring, and twisting her stomach into knots that could make dining difficult.

Breathing deep did her sensory glands a whole load of good and made her smile back at him. 'We'll have a good time regardless.' She was determined to. It wasn't often she got to go to a fancy dinner with a gorgeous man at her side to help raise funds for a worthwhile cause. Let's face it, she'd never done anything like this. Making the most of Kristof's mother's generous gesture wasn't going to be hard. 'Where's your mother?'

'Over the other side of the room working the crowd. When it comes to her strays, she's very good at getting people to put their hands in their pockets, or wave their credit cards over a machine.' Pride was mixed with resentment in his voice, in the tightness rippling off his shoulders.

What had he missed out on that he resented his mother giving so much of herself to those children? 'Has she always run the shelter? Or is it something she's started recently?'

Kristof took two glasses of champagne from the hovering waiter and passed one to her before sitting down. 'I thought we were talking about your travels.'

Shut down just like that. Go with it or up the ante? She glanced at Kristof's profile; his jutting jaw warned best to go with him if this evening was to be the fun she'd decided to have. Though that jaw was quite sexy with its implied strength and determination. 'I arrived in England two years ago with a six-month contract in the children's ward in Bristol's main hospital. While there I bought a car so I could get out and see places. At the end of that job I went to Wales for another short-term position.'

He listened with an intensity that seemed to cut out everyone and all the noise around them. Warmth stole over her. No man had shown such courtesy, or even interest, in her exploits before. Usually they only ever wanted to talk about themselves.

'Go on.'

It wasn't happening. His mother appeared between them and leaned down to kiss Alesha on both cheeks. 'Thank you for coming.

I'm sure you'll have a wonderful evening. Now I'd like to introduce you to the other guests seated with us.'

When Alesha glanced behind this formidable woman she saw three couples waiting to be shown to their seats. She stood up at the same time as Kristof.

He placed his hand on her waist in a proprietary manner and nodded to everyone, taking over from his mother. 'Hello, everyone. This is Alesha, a nurse from New Zealand who's on holiday in Dubrovnik. Alesha, I'd like you to meet Filip and Nina Babic.'

As her hand was warmly shaken Alesha smiled and hoped everyone spoke a little English, but if not then she'd still enjoy the ambiance. Handshaking over, everyone sat and soon the noise level had increased to deafening.

Kristof leaned in close. 'Not sorry you came?'

She shook her head, breathed in his spicy aftershave, and smiled. 'If that's your get out of jail card, then sorry, but this is fun.'

'How much are you understanding?' He grinned.

'Very little but I'm fine with that, though I will need you to interpret the menu.' She could see it lying by her setting and it was impossible to read.

'Be nice to me or I'll extract revenge.' His breath was warm on her neck.

She could go with his revenge if that meant getting closer. Looking around, because looking at Kristof was too disturbing, she was shocked to find everyone with them was watching her and Kristof with indulgent smiles on their faces. 'Kristof,' she hissed into his ear. 'Sit up.'

He did, slowly, and gave her a wide smile before turning to talk to the woman on his other side.

On her right Filip asked, 'Have you come all the way from New Zealand to see our city?'

At least that was what she thought he asked in his scrambled English. His effort was appreciated. Any English was better than her Croatian. 'Not quite. I've been living in England for two years, visiting different European countries as work allows.' This was getting repetitive.

'You're fortunate you can do this.'

'I am,' she replied and sneaked a look at Kristof, who was watching her with a speculative gleam in his eyes. 'What?' A delicate shiver strolled up her spine.

'Nothing. Just keeping an eye out for you in what must be a strange setting.'

He had her back? She also couldn't remember anyone doing that for her before. She'd been mixing with the wrong crowds. Kristof was setting her a new benchmark. Not that she'd be getting any ideas regarding her and Kristof. Tonight was only about enjoying the moment, and this moment was with Kristof and his mother's friends. Turning to Filip, she told him, 'Having no ties back home allows me the pleasure of travelling wherever I choose.'

'You don't have family?'

She shook her head. Not really. Not one that acknowledged her, at any rate. 'No.'

'*Djèca?*'

'Pardon?'

'He means do you have any children?' Kristof spoke over his shoulder.

The guy was involved in another conversation and listening in on hers at the same time? She needed to be careful around him. Focusing on Filip, she said, 'I don't have a partner so no children.' Having children of her own would be wonderful and something she hoped for in the future. She'd love them unreservedly, never push them away or make them feel unwanted. Never.

Kristof turned his attention back to her. 'This guy who called off your relationship the other week? How serious were you about him?'

She preferred it when Kristof had his back

to her. While this had nothing to do with him, she answered anyway. 'I wouldn't have agreed to come here with him if I wasn't.' But was that really true? It had been the romance of the occasion that had sucked her in, excited her, because no other man had ever promised such an exciting wonderful holiday for her, with her.

Kristof nodded. 'Fair enough.'

'Everyone has their way of showing their feelings,' she snapped, shaken at the idea seeping into her thoughts over the past couple of days. She was more angry about once again being shown she was unlovable than feeling as if her heart had been ripped out of her chest.

A large, warm hand covered hers briefly, those long fingers squeezing gently. 'You're right. I'm sorry.'

'Kristof.' She aimed for serous, half got it right. 'I'm not grieving for him. I'm angry he let me down, and for thinking there was more to our relationship than was real.' Startled, she dropped her fork. That was so true.

'Enough. Enjoy your entrée.' Kristof removed his hand, and picked up a fork. 'I hope you like lobster.'

Her mouth salivated. 'Do I what?' Grinning, she forked up a healthy mouthful. 'One of my favourite foods of all time. What else are we having?'

'Next course is rabbit goulash, followed by an apple and chocolate creation I'm sure you'll love.' His smile was wicked, sending her stomach into a riot of butterflies.

As the night progressed Alesha found it harder and harder to keep on track. Whenever Kristof looked at her as though *she* was his favourite course all her defence mechanisms came into play, at the same time warring with the need to have fun and follow her determination to enjoy each day as it unfolded. This latest version of her week in Dubrovnik had her blood racing and her nerves out of kilter. What if she made another mistake so soon after the last one? Was she throwing herself at Kristof?

Have a fling.

How did she start one if not by showing her intentions?

'We're only spending the evening together helping my mother out,' Kristof said in a tone that spoke loud and clear—there'd be no further dates. A reminder he hadn't been the one to invite her here.

Apparently she was an open book. 'I wasn't expecting anything else.' Although she might have been wishing for more. Disappointment tugged, because she was out with a handsome man in an amazing setting in a city far from any other she'd visited, and of course it would be fun to experience *everything* the city had to offer.

'Good.' This man did blunt well.

Time for a subject change. She shoved her chair back. 'I'm going to look at the gifts to be auctioned.' Bidding for something would be the right thing to do after Kristof's mother had so kindly invited her along.

Kristof strolled alongside her, his shoulder brushing hers. Intentionally? After his warning? There were mixed messages coming her way. 'There's lots of art; paintings, pottery, and sketches. Most are too big to carry back to London.'

'Tell me what those vouchers are for.' Alesha pointed to a line of cards with photos of food, buses, views, and a beauty parlour, trying to ignore his tall, well-proportioned body. 'I get what most of them are about, but not where the service offered is situated. Like that one.' Her finger tapped a picture of an outdoor restaurant with the sparkling blue ocean as a backdrop.

'Cavtat, which is south of here. You can go by road, or, better yet, take a boat ride down there. It's a lovely town with a baroque church and the Rector's Palace to visit. The beaches are stunning, and there are lots of food choices.'

'You've sold me on the place. I'll visit one day this week.' She'd bid for that voucher, even though it was a meal for two people. She laughed. Perhaps she could use it twice. Or talk Kristof into going with her. Although, he'd made it clear, no further dates, remember? Was this even a date when his mother had invited her and demanded Kristof drive her?

'You could eat there every night this week for what you've just bid,' Kristof admonished an hour later when she held the Cavtat restaurant voucher in her hand.

'That's hardly the point of this auction.'

'I doubt my mother invited you along to spend your hard-earned money.'

'Then why did she?' Alesha asked, doubting she'd get an answer.

Kristof's face softened. 'She likes making kind gestures. Genuinely kind ones.'

And that was all Alesha was getting. She could ask until she was blue in the face but Kristof would not say another word on the subject. She knew that shut-off look already. She recognised the need to keep himself to himself, because it was the same with her. It didn't stop her wanting to wipe away that hurt flitting through his eyes, pain that he thought he had under wraps. 'Would you like to come to this restaurant with me?'

'I don't think that's a good idea.'

'I'm not asking you to do anything you wouldn't want to, just to share another meal with me.' So far she'd been in Dubrovnik two nights and had eaten with Kristof for both of them. 'Let me know if you change your mind.'

'I could drive you down to Cavtat after I finish at the children's centre, I suppose.'

Sound happy about it, why don't you?

'I'm going by boat so I get to see the coast along the way.' Sitting on a ferry was far more fun than in a car. 'Or don't you like being on the water?'

'You're persistent, aren't you?' He finally cracked a smile that sent fire throughout her. 'Okay, thank you. I'll go with you by boat to Cavtat. As long as we walk around the peninsula before eating. It's a spectacular spot with the water so clear you can see right to the bottom.'

'Done.' She wouldn't look smug, or excited, or grateful. Nope, just relieved, and happy, and—calm. Okay, that wasn't so easy to pull off, but she gave it her best shot. 'I guess we're going for dinner, not lunch?'

'Yes. If that's all right with you?' Kristof hastened to add, inexplicable excitement flashing across his face before he shut down again.

What was that about? Forget the fling idea.

It wasn't happening. They both had too many issues to let loose and enjoy each other. 'Absolutely.'

He stood up and reached for her hand to pull her gently upright. 'Let's say goodnight to everyone and get out of here. I've done my bit for this time.'

There it was again, that hint he was not happy about something to do with his mother. Or was it her charity he had issues with? Yet he gave her weeks out of what would no doubt be a hectic schedule back in London. Alesha smoothed down the front of her dress and looked at Kristof as he said goodbye to Filip and Nina. She'd probably never know what made this man tick. That wasn't such a bad thing. After this week she wouldn't see him again anyway. Getting to know more about him only meant getting close, involved with him, and she didn't need that. Nor, she suspected, did he.

Outside in the slightly cooler air Alesha stared around at the city so alien to anything at home. The night lights and shadows gave an eerie yet exhilarating feel to the place. 'Wow.'

'Come on. I'll take you down to the harbour edge. It's on the other side of these buildings.' Kristof reached for her hand.

The need to slip her hand in his was strong. As was the need to kiss him. She did neither. The champagne had been delicious at dinner but she'd refrained from enjoying too much, and she could do the same about holding hands. It would only be a gesture and she didn't need any more of those now that she'd made up her mind to be strong—and single.

Kristof pulled off the road outside the apartment complex, relieved he'd got Alesha back without giving into the temptation that was her scent, her beauty, the wondrous figure that skin-tight dress highlighted, her soft yet strong voice. He'd lost count of how many times he'd made to haul her into his arms so he could kiss her down at the waterfront by the boats tied up. Temptation usually came with written warnings, but there were no warnings about Alesha.

None other than the ones his brain kept throwing up. What really bugged him was that he never hesitated when a woman came on to him, and yet last night when Alesha had he'd hauled the brakes on fast. She overwhelmed him with her smiles, her frankness.

Oh, get real. She's so sexy in that little red number it's impossible to ignore her.

He wanted her, plain and simple.

Alesha opened her door. 'Thanks for a great time. I'll see you later in the week.'

Cavtat. Why had he agreed to go with her? How could he not when she'd looked at him with such candour in those heart-stopping eyes and said it was only for a meal? That felt like a challenge, and challenges were not to be ignored. 'I'll call to let you know what night works with my programme at the children's home.'

'I'm going to spend time with Capeka again so I might see you there.' She clambered out of the car. 'Goodnight, Kristof.'

No way. Alesha wasn't getting away that easily. The brakes were off. He wanted her. 'Wait.' He held his hand out for the keys. 'Let me.'

'It isn't necessary,' she quipped. 'I usually only make an idiot of myself once over any one thing.'

'Humour me, okay? One thing I did learn growing up was manners.' And to work hard at being different from his father. But that was another story, which had nothing to do with what was going on in his body.

'You just don't want to find me sleeping on the side of the road when you go to work in the morning.' Somehow she managed to pass the keys to him without touching his skin.

'I'll bring some toast in case.' The sorry dope he'd suddenly turned into had been hoping for a little bit of contact, an indication she might be a little attracted to him.

Her laughter tinkled in the clear air, drew him closer to her as they climbed the steps up to the apartments. His gaze fell to the curved, swaying backside in front of him, his groin tightening alarmingly. He should've stayed in the car. Then they were on the level and Alesha was waiting for him to open the door to her apartment, her back to him.

'Who's going to undo that zip for you?' The words spilled out. A logical question considering he'd had to finish doing up the zip in the first place, but it was filled with suggestion and hope and need that he couldn't hide. When had he last felt so awkward with a woman? Probably when he'd asked Melissa Stokes to his sixth birthday party.

'I could go door knocking,' she tossed over her shoulder as she stepped inside.

He followed her in and reached for her, hands on her shoulders. 'I don't like that idea.'

'Really? Then what are you going to do about it?'

Slowly he turned her around and lifted those long waves of golden brown hair with one hand. With the other he nudged the zip down an inch. And another inch. Another. All the way to the top of those curves he'd followed up the steps. The air stuck in his throat at the beauty before him. Soft, satin-like skin the colour of vanilla ice cream. The gentle flaring of those hips shaping her dress. The heat, the scent of summer. Everything about Alesha made his body hum.

Oh, so slowly Alesha turned. His hand spread across the width of the small of her back, the other cradling her hair, letting the silky texture slide through his fingers. The last of the restraints he'd placed on himself during the evening evaporated in an instant of heat and desire. Gone. All he knew was he wanted her so badly it hurt in places pain had no right to be. He leaned down so his mouth could caress Alesha's. It wasn't enough. Her soft lips melted into his so they became one where their mouths joined. It wasn't enough. His hands slid under the fabric of her dress, slid it down over her shoulders, while at the same time he kicked the door closed.

Alesha hesitated, pulled back to lock an unsteady gaze on him.

His lungs stalled.

Please don't say no.

Then she smiled and her lips were returning to his, her tongue making forays into his fevered mouth, driving him crazy. If this was what kissing Alesha did to him, then the next hour was going to be unbelievably erotic.

A low, slow groan escaped her mouth as she pressed her breasts against his chest, her taut nipples like beads of desire throbbing with the beat of his blood. He wound his arms tighter, brought her so close they moulded together. It was wonderful. The heat, the need coursing through his veins, and, he knew, hers too. It wasn't enough. His shirt and her dress were impediments.

Setting Alesha back only as far as necessary, he nudged the narrow straps from her shoulders. The dress fell away. Nothing held those pert breasts, no lace or silk, nothing but nature. His knees bowed. As he reached to bring her up against him she resisted.

'I want to see you.' Her hands were tugging his shirt free of his trousers.

He took his hands away from that warm skin for the moment it took to drag the offending garment over his head and toss it aside. Then he went back to touching, holding, looking. Feeling, aching, needing. And lifting her into his arms to place her on the beckoning bed where he could make love with this amazing woman all night long. Where he would give her everything she needed and wanted, first.

Where the pleasure would be as much his as hers. Where he could lose himself in her heat, and her generosity.

CHAPTER FIVE

ALESHA ROLLED OVER in the rumpled mess that was sheets and pillows and the heady smell of a night making love with Kristof, and dragged her eyes open. Some time after the sun came up he had left to go back to his mother's house to get ready for a day at the children's home. He hadn't kissed her goodbye, hadn't uttered a word, just slipped into his shirt and trousers, slung his jacket over his shoulder and left. Message clear—this had been a one-off night.

It was surprising how comfortable she was with that. It might be too soon after being dumped but she'd gone into the evening eyes wide open and mind clear about having fun without any attachments. Her heart had not been involved, nor was it going to become so. Just because they'd both wanted to have fun without consequences that didn't make them a couple, or even best friends.

Shuffling up the bed and stuffing a pillow

behind her, she leaned back and looked around. Sunlight snuck around the edges of the wooden blinds, teasing her to get up and make the most of another bright and sunny day. In a minute. It was relaxing to sit here with nowhere she had to be by a specific time. Freedom from work. Freedom from other people's expectations. Living up to her own for a change. Feeling hollowed out, yes, but that came with a sense of getting to understand herself as never before.

Looking back, she saw the nine-year-old version of Alesha—sad, bewildered, lost. Her parents suddenly didn't have time to talk to her about school or the games she played as they'd done before. They withdrew their love so she went looking for it elsewhere. Which was where this chasing men came from, she recognised now. She plucked at the sheet, unable to cry for the child who'd become the woman she was now, her heart heavy. Yet persistent hope pinged her. This time it was hope she'd get her life sorted in a way that fitted with her new dreams. Be strong and— She faltered. And single? Was it Kristof who'd made her see things differently? If so, she owed him, and not in a clingy, 'let's be together' kind of way.

There'd been a certain freedom about the evening, followed by that sexy, sensual night, with a man she'd only met the day before. Having never done anything so unrestrained before she'd have thought remorse would've been her prime emotion today, but no. For the first time in a long time she was completely relaxed, wasn't looking for hints of what might come in the future, what Kristof might expect of her today or next week or even when they were back in London. For once she wasn't getting ahead of herself.

Untangling her legs from the sheet, she leapt out of bed and stretched up on tiptoes, arms above her head, then bent to touch the floor with her fingers. While muscles everywhere ached, her body felt alive and ready for action. More action. Like a swim, breakfast, a visit to see Capeka, and then walk into the Old City to take a mini-tour up to the lookout on the hills behind the city.

'Morning,' Karolina called from the other side of the deck where she was sweeping the moment Alesha walked outside dressed in her bikini. 'You had a good time last night?'

How much did she know? 'I had a great time. The auction was a huge success.'

'So I hear.' Karolina's eyes sparkled with mischief.

So she knew more than how the dinner had gone. No need to confirm or deny though.

Placing her keys and phone on a sunbed, Alesha then dived into the sparkling water and popped up at the far end. 'How often does Antonija organise auctions? I gather last night's wasn't the first.'

'Once a year. She says any more wouldn't bring in more money and double the cost of putting them on.'

'That makes sense.' As far as Alesha could discern, if ever there was a sensible woman Kristof's mother was her. 'The children's home must cost a bit to run.'

'I think so. Though Kristof arranges for doctors to come from England throughout the year free of charge.'

So he was happy to help out but had issues about his mother. She was not about to ask Karolina anything about him. That gleam in those knowing eyes would only increase and she didn't need that. She also wasn't going to explain she was having a week like no other where she'd be free and happy and take whatever was on offer, then go back to England, sign up for another job. Which reminded her—that job Cherry called about. She'd send in an application before she got on with this new way of life.

Oh, boy. She had plenty to think about. But not now. Job application, then a shower before heading down the hill for breakfast at one of those bakeries she'd spied yesterday on her way back from Port Gruž.

'Morning, Alesha,' Kristof called from the other end of the hallway as she entered the building. 'I didn't expect you here quite so soon.'

I didn't expect my pulse to go from slow to racing in two seconds flat just seeing you.

'Hi. Thought I'd spend some time with Capeka before I go sightseeing, if that's all right?' Had Kristof been looking out for her? Unlikely after his quiet way of leaving her apartment that morning. 'I'd like to try reading to her again, but only if you think it won't distress her when I'm leaving at the end of the week.'

'My mother was hoping you'd drop in for that reason, so she's not concerned about Capeka getting too fond of you in a short time.'

'That's good.' Alesha's heart rate sped up as she studied this man she'd been so intimate with before knowing much about him. But she had known he was kind, helpful, considerate, could laugh, and smiled like every woman's dream. What more did she need to know? He hadn't hurt her, probably wouldn't either. He certainly wouldn't if she didn't let him close. Did she regret last night? Not one bit.

'Got a minute first? I'd like to ask you a couple of things.' Kristof held a hand out in the direction of a door along the hall.

'Sure.' Nothing about last night showed in his straight expression. None of the passion or need or even the delight in sharing what they'd had. They were back to friendly without over-doing it. 'Sure,' she repeated.

She'd barely parked her butt on the chair by a desk when he asked, 'What line of nursing are you most qualified in?'

Definitely back to basics. That was fine by her. 'I've mostly worked on children's wards and in paediatric ICU. But as all nurses do in their training, I've covered everything and feel comfortable in most situations. Why?'

'Theatre work?'

So that was where this was going. 'Yes, some, but not for eighteen months when I worked for five weeks as a fill-in at one of the East London hospitals.'

Kristof locked his intense gaze on her. 'I know you're on holiday so this is asking a lot, but we're down a theatre nurse today and I have a tight schedule of small surgeries.' He paused. 'Would you mind helping with hand-ing over bandages, suture equipment, things like that?'

Alesha rushed in. 'No problem.' The tour

would be on every day so she wasn't missing out on anything and if she was needed here then that was fine with her.

'It's mundane, I know, but you haven't got clearance to work as a qualified nurse. I'd still like to check your credentials though.'

'I'd be leery if you didn't. Ring the nursing employment agency I am currently working through.' She tapped her phone for the number, and gave him a name to ask for. 'While you're doing that I'll go say hello to Capeka. Oh, and mundane doesn't bother me if I'm helping someone.'

Kristof was already picking up the phone, barely giving her a nod.

Okay. Definitely professional mode. Did that mean last night never happened? Or he wanted to forget it had? Or was Kristof afraid she was expecting more? Hearing him ask for the recruitment manager she'd referred him to, Alesha gave a mental shrug and left him to it. Whatever he thought about their night together wasn't going to change her plans.

Heading to the classroom where she'd met Capeka yesterday, she found a happy smile before entering quietly so as not to disturb the children who were all engrossed in their books. All, except one wee girl standing in the corner on one leg.

Alesha said hello to the teacher, and instantly Capeka lifted her head, a glimmer of hope in those big, sad eyes.

Oh, oh. This might not be a wise idea if the child was starting to look out for her. But Kristof said his mother was happy for her to drop by and if she could do even the smallest amount of good for this girl she would.

The teacher was holding out a book towards Alesha and she took it, relieved to see it was another classic that she could semi interpret into English. Not that it mattered if she made up the whole story since Capeka wouldn't understand a word, but it felt more right somehow.

Settling onto a small chair near without being too close to Capeka, she opened the book and dug into early childhood memories of sitting on her mother's knee to listen to this story. The words came readily. As did the warmth and security of being with her mother. Too readily. Her voice faltered. Deep breath, carry on. This was about a child in need right before her, not about *her*. Nor was it anything to do with what had happened when she'd been a child. But for the first time in a long time Alesha admitted to herself that she had a longing for those days when she'd been safe and loved and totally secure in her little girl's life.

Read, damn it. *Just* read. As in make up words to fit the pictures on the pages.

A small hand touched her arm, withdrew immediately.

Raising her eyes, Alesha saw an understanding in the brown eyes staring at her. An understanding no child this age should have. It was desperately hard not to reach out and hug this girl tight. Capeka had heard her pain in her voice and reacted. In the kindest way.

How am I going to leave her at the end of the week?

It might be kinder never to see her again than do that.

The girl stood in front of her, closer than she'd been before, one leg tucked tight behind the other, her arms folded across her waist. Her face was blank, but in those eyes a score of emotions swirled. Good, bad and probably the ugly. Then Capeka dipped her head as though to say, 'Come on. Keep reading.'

So she did.

Until the sound of a man clearing his throat interrupted. Kristof stood near but not so near as to frighten Capeka, watching them both. His eyes were unreadable.

Alesha asked, 'Did I pass muster?'

An abrupt nod. 'Of course. When you've finished that book I'd like to get started in

Theatre. There are things I'll need to explain and show you first.'

'I'll be five minutes.' Returning to the story, she noted he didn't leave, merely stood there, watching and listening, and in a glance she saw just as unfathomable as he'd been earlier. His professional face. The one he seemed to use all the time around here. Thank goodness he hadn't used it last night or they'd never have got far.

Kristof's professionalism continued throughout the day. 'First up is a tonsillectomy. Mila is five and has had constant throat infections for the last nine months as far as we're aware. They probably go back a lot further but we only met her last September. Other children I'm operating on today have come in from the surrounding country towns where there are no hospitals. By coming to us they're avoiding the long waiting lists in the cities.'

'Does the children's home get funding for these operations?' she asked, without thinking she was probably overstepping the mark with such a question.

Kristof gave her one sharp shake of his handsome head. Scrubbed up and dressed in clean operating garb, he still looked as sexy as it was possible for a man to be. More than.

Alesha smiled behind her mask, let the heat

that thought caused absorb into her, went with the job on hand, helping the other nurse as required. Stepping up to the table where Mila lay anaesthetised, she said, 'She's a little cutie, for sure.'

'A vast improvement on the day she came to us,' Jacob, the anaesthetist, informed her. An older man who worked part time at the local hospital, he was apparently always available for operations in this Theatre.

'Then I'm hoping Capeka will one day be happy too.'

'There's a long way to go before that's possible,' Kristof muttered, glancing her way, a snap heatwave blasting the air between them. Not so professional now, was he?

Gotcha.

She grinned behind her mask.

His gaze dropped to the top of her scrubs where her breasts resided, his eyes widening.

Her nipples tightened. Oh, boy, trouble in scrubs. Alesha grabbed the box of wipes the other nurse was indicating and dragged her eyes away from the man who'd given her the night of her life. Today was going to take for ever to end.

Kristof lifted a scalpel. 'Here we go.'

Alesha was in awe of the surgeon from that moment on. Not just the man under the scrubs. Kristof was focused on one thing and one thing only, removing Mila's tonsils with as little trauma as possible. He was thorough, tidy, neat with his suturing, fast to keep the time under anaesthesia to a minimum. In other words the best surgeon she'd ever had the privilege to observe in Theatre.

No surprises there, she realised as she donned another set of scrubs for their next patient—another tonsillectomy. Followed by the breaking and resetting of a small boy's fractured arm that had not been put in a cast at the time the injury occurred three months earlier. That made Alesha shiver. Even though she'd come across a similar case years ago it was still hard to believe a child could go without medical help. A child deserved all the kindness and care available out there, no matter where they lived or who they lived with. But that was being Pollyanna-ish, and she knew she wasn't about to change the world. At least she was helping a few youngsters in Dubrovnik.

When they stopped for a quick cup of tea and sandwich Kristof read files and absently put food in his mouth.

Alesha watched him from under lowered eyebrows, though she probably could've stared hard at him and he wouldn't have noticed.

Then he looked up and she realised he knew

she'd been studying him. He nodded and returned to his notes.

Soon they returned to Theatre for an appendectomy, followed by other small but essential surgeries. The worst came in as they were wrapping up for the day. A boy had been attacked by a dog, his arm torn apart as he'd apparently tried to hide his face. In that, he'd succeeded, with only scratches on his cheeks. But the trauma they had to deal with was hideous and it would be a long time before the lad would be using his arm to full potential again, if ever.

'Why wasn't he taken to the main hospital?' Alesha asked.

'I don't know,' Kristof replied, not looking at her.

But he was guessing, and not liking what he was coming up with. She wouldn't probe any further. They'd been there to help the boy and that was all that mattered. Since this seemed to be the only room to change in, she slipped out of her scrubs pants and stepped into her sky-blue capris. 'I'm glad you could put him back together.' The odds on the boy's recovery being good were vastly improved having had Kristof operate on him.

'So am I.' Kristof had taken both pieces of

his scrubs off and was pulling on khaki knee-length shorts, followed by a white tee shirt.

She tried not to gape at the array of muscles filling her vision with only the boxers to cover some of them. She quickly gave up and enjoyed the view. After all, he could've waited until she left the room before stripping down to his underwear, but, then again, she'd seen it all anyway. Did this mean professional Kristof was back in his box and the fun guy was joining her? Letting her hair free of the thick band she'd tugged it into earlier, she dragged a brush through the tangle. 'I'm going to see Capeka before heading out into the sunshine.' She presumed it was still sunny outside.

'I'll walk you back to the apartments when you're ready.' Kristof was studying his fingers. Then he raised his head and hit her with an irresistible smile. 'Can't have you getting lost or locked out.'

Right then she'd have done anything he asked. *Anything.* That smile should be bottled and sold to raise funds for this place. Her knees were incapable of bending, her head spun, and as for her heart—it had obviously forgotten what it had been put inside her chest to do. 'As if,' she croaked through a mire of happy shock.

'We'll go to Cavtat tonight.' He checked his watch. 'How about you have half an hour with

Capeka then we'll head up the hill to get ready, and I'll pick you up at six?' That smile just got wider and warmer and—oh, where was the professional guy when she needed him?

'Umm, yes, I suppose so.' Wasn't she the one with the restaurant voucher? 'I thought I'd like to go by boat, remember?'

'I do. I'll arrange that. But we'll drive down to the Old City. It's a bit of a walk home from the boat after a late night.'

Alesha's face was worth a thousand pictures. Kristof had watched as excitement followed by irritation then resignation vied for supremacy. All because he'd taken charge about when to go to Cavtat. 'I figured since it's looking like being a beautiful evening we should make the most of it.' The chances of rain any time throughout the week were non-existent, but still. He hadn't been able to get any part of the previous evening and night out of his blood, out of his head, so the sooner they had this dinner together, the better. By the end of the night he'd either be over Ms Alesha Milligan or hanging out for more time with her. He had a sneaking suspicion which it would be after feasting his eyes on her most of the long day in Theatre.

Glancing at his watch, he grimaced. How long did thirty minutes take?

Apparently for ever. It wasn't as though Alesha had dragged out her time with Capeka. In fact it'd been bang on half an hour when she'd put aside the book she'd been using to make up a story to go with the pictures and left the room. 'Ready when you are,' she told him.

Was she as keen as him for the evening to begin? He hadn't felt this excited about a date in so long it was ridiculous. It had to be the air, or the sun, or the fact he was away from London. Yeah right. Try the red bikini, or that stunning figure, or the generosity in Alesha's lovemaking. Any one of those would do it. Put them all together and what chance did he have to remain sane and sensible around her? But he had to try. 'The boat ride's booked.'

'I'm looking forward to it,' she replied, sounding less excited than him.

'You're sure? We could make it another night.'

Don't dare say that's a good idea.

Was he rushing her? Into what? A dinner date that she'd asked him on. That was all. Relief softened his worry. He hadn't signed up for life. Didn't have to face the consequences of being tied to a woman for ever. The relief increased. He was just showing her some of the sights of his second hometown, as any decent person would. She'd been let down by the man who'd arranged this trip. In his book she deserved better than that. It wasn't as though he intended spending a lot of time with Alesha. Come Saturday he was on his way back to London.

As Alesha would be, he reminded himself. So what? They wouldn't have anything to do with each other there. They moved in different circles, professionally and privately. The only way they'd bump into each other would be if one of them deliberately got in touch with the other. And that was not happening. Not when he didn't trust women not to play around on him or rip him off or hurt him in some other way. He'd given his heart once, got it back flattened and broken. This wasn't only about Alesha. Most people he got close to just didn't seem able to give him what he wanted—honest to goodness friendship and commitment. Nothing more, nothing less. Not even his parents had done that.

'Tonight's good. I've got to grab the opportunity while I can. Who knows what I might find to do tomorrow night?' Alesha's smile was light and general, not aimed to knock him sideways.

But it did. He could live on Alesha smiles. They were warm, sometimes sexy, and always slapped his heart. Which wasn't good—but felt wonderful. 'Then let's head up the hill to get ready.' If she'd changed her mind about wanting to go with him to use her dinner voucher then she'd have to tell him. He wasn't going to make it easy for her to back off when he was looking out for her.

Tonight's figure-hugging dress was navy blue and as tantalising as the red one had been. More so now that Kristof knew what was underneath. For a guy who wasn't interested in getting close to a woman his body had other ideas, mocking his carefully held theories on how to live his life safely. 'You look beautiful,' he told Alesha as they strode along the wharf to their ride to Cavtat.

'Thank you.' Her tone was demure but her eyes were sparkling with pleasure.

'You also look happy.' She'd rallied quickly after being tossed aside for another woman. Or was she good at hiding her feelings? Except last night she hadn't held back in bed. He'd swear she'd made love to him with no thoughts for any other man.

'It's a wonderful city and I'm enjoying it,

plus your company.' Then the smile dropped and she shrugged. 'You think I'm not acting how I should be after what Luke did to me.'

Kristof stopped and reached for both her hands. 'I'm thinking let's have a fling for the days we're both in Dubrovnik.'

The smile didn't return as her stunned gaze locked on him. 'Are you serious?'

'Yes.' Now that he thought about it, he was. Very. 'I know this week hasn't started out how you'd expected and I don't intend trying to make up for that. But last night was fun, and I like your company.' He shrugged. 'So why not? It can't hurt anyone.'

Her head flicked back, fell forward. 'As far as proposals go that's very sterile.' Then she lifted her chin, focused her gaze back on him. 'But I like that. It's perfect really. Originally I was coming here for fun and romance, instead I can have fun and—and more fun.' Her shoulders lifted deliberately.

'Hey, any time you're not happy say so and we'll call it quits.'

Finally she relaxed. 'Works for me.'

Worked for him and all. 'Then let's get on that boat before it leaves without us.' He kept one of her soft hands wrapped in his large one as he strode along the wharf. 'You're going to love Cavtat.'

* * *

Alesha wiped her mouth with the napkin and placed it beside her empty plate. 'That walnut torte is to die for.'

Kristof laughed. 'Told you. Like some more wine?'

She shook her head. 'No, thanks.' One night overindulging had been one too many. If they were going to bed together later on she wanted to be fully aware of everything, of Kristof. She did not want to miss a thing about that hard body and talented mouth, those sensuous fingers and cheeky lips. So she *was* having a fling. Who better to start this new lifestyle of having fun and no involvement with than a hunk who knew more about making love—sorry, having sex—than she'd have thought possible? Showed the kind of men she'd known before. They hadn't been up to scratch at all. Whereas Kristof had reset the line. Spoiled her for ever, probably. At least she'd have some amazing holiday memories. Just not the ones she'd expected.

'It's a pity you wore those shoes or we could've walked around the peninsula.'

'Isn't the path paved?' She'd forgotten about the walk when she'd been preening herself for the evening.

'Unfortunately not.'

'Then I'll have to come back in the day time because I do want to go around there and sit down by the water.' It would have been wonderful at night with Kristof, but this was a fling, not something romantic, so the shoes had saved her from getting her old hopes up.

'You should do that. There are also some buildings in the township to check out.' He didn't seem perturbed at having missed out on a night stroll with her. 'Are you into kayaking?'

'It's been a while but, yes, I could hire one and take a look at the town from out on the harbour.' Another day sorted. 'Tomorrow I am going to take that mini tour up the hill and on to the waterfall.'

'You'll love it.'

'Unless you need me at the children's centre again?' She'd be just as happy working alongside Kristof.

He stood up and reached for her hand, pulled her chair out as she rose. 'No, Alesha. You're here to see the sights and have already lost a day for the kids, so go out and make the most of the days you have left.'

Not mentioning the nights? 'I'll find time to read to Capeka though.'

'Don't feel bad if you find you're busy having fun and run out of time for a visit. She's still settling in and getting lots of attention from everyone else.'

So the reading times weren't important? Alesha thought otherwise. 'I'm sure I can find half an hour for her.' Unless she was causing more harm than good, but so far no one thought she was.

'Do you always let people close so quickly?' Kristof asked once they'd left the restaurant and were strolling down towards the harbour and their boat ride back to the city.

Did she? To a point, maybe. 'I like to be open with people.' Was he referring to Capeka? Or himself? 'Capeka needs people to care about what happens to her, and I want to give her some little thing to help her on that journey.'

She wasn't doing this for herself. Or was she? Could this be a way to avoid thinking too much about how much she'd hoped there was a future for her and Luke? But now she understood she hadn't been decimated by his news. She'd been hurt, angry, let down—all of the above. But heartbroken? Deep breath. Really gutted to the point she hadn't been able to get out of bed to face the next day? No, not even immediately after he'd told her. Kristof was probably rebound sex. But hey, if that was what it was so be it. It had helped, been fun, enjoyable, and she didn't feel ashamed at all. Kristof had made it all so easy. He'd had fun too, and that was that. Very civilised. Funny how bitter her laugh tasted.

'You need to guard your heart, or one day you're going to get hurt badly.'

Did he really just say that? Kristof, the man who was serious at work, and fun at play? She stared at him. He was wearing that professional look that grated, as though this was something he'd talk about but not on a personal level. So he'd been hurt in the past too. Find a normal adult who hadn't in one way or another to a varying degree. 'My heart's safe.'

'Then Luke didn't mean as much to you as I thought.'

'Maybe he's why it's safe.' Or the guy before him, or the one before that.

Kristof's arm was deliciously heavy over her shoulders, and she liked that she could tuck against his side and not look into those eyes that didn't miss a thing.

'What's your past, Alesha?'

Go for the big question, why don't you?

'Oh, I don't know. Unlucky in love?'

'A commitment-phobe?'

'It wasn't me who finished my last relationship. Or any of the others.'

'That doesn't really answer my question.

You might be putting men off with a "you can look and touch but you can't keep" attitude.'

'And here I thought you were a surgeon.' Not an analyst who believed he could unravel her. 'Are you basing these questions on your past experiences?'

The muscles in his arm tensed on her shoulders. 'It's possible.'

They reached the jetty and joined the queue to board their return trip. There was no way they'd continue the discussion when surrounded by happy couples and groups laughing and making lots of noise. Instead they stood at the bow of the boat, Kristof using his body to shelter her from the cooler breeze created by the boat's forward motion, holding her close, his arms wrapped around her, his hands linked at her waist. Snuggling back against him, Alesha went with the moment, not thinking about tomorrow or next week or anything other than the lights on the hills they passed on the way back to Dubrovnik. Wasn't that the free and easy way to go?

Meandering through the Old City after disembarking, Alesha sighed with pleasure. A simple night out, no complexities, no one demanding more of her than she was prepared to give. There was something warming, and comfortable, and just plain lovely about it all.

Something she didn't remember experiencing in any relationship in the past. Usually men expected more of her than they gave back.

Yes, and whose fault was that?

She'd gone along with them because she'd believed it was the way to a man's heart. Now she was starting to see how wrong she might've been. This going it alone wasn't such a bad idea at all. It meant she had begun standing up for herself. Another first.

When Kristof pulled his car into a park outside the apartments where she was staying it wasn't hard for Alesha to ask, 'Do you want to come in?'

'Yes.'

Her heart swelled and her body warmed. As far as flings went this was great. And they didn't have to talk, just hold each other and touch and feel and give and take…

CHAPTER SIX

IF THE DAYS sped past, the nights went even quicker. Alesha toured the city, the outlying environs, many of the islands nearby. She ate in bakeries, cafés, and at night enjoyed restaurants with Kristof. She told stories to Capeka every day, sometimes twice a day, and Friday, the day before she was leaving for London, the little girl gave her a smile filled with nothing but pleasure, which showed the lack of understanding of each other's language meant absolutely nothing. They were on the same page.

'Seeing her smile directly at me, her eyes meeting mine for the first time…it just blew me away,' she told Kristof over a quick coffee before heading into town. 'Now we need to get her to stop standing on one foot in the corner.'

'You're getting too involved,' he warned. 'Be careful.'

'Your mother's monitoring everything and I don't believe for one minute she'd let me visit

if she thought it was detrimental for Capeka.'
They still didn't know the girl's real name, or
where she'd come from before arriving at the
bridge. Apparently this wasn't unusual in similar cases. Alesha could understand the child
not wanting to trust anyone with information
about herself. People could use it in ways that
hurt, and given how young Capeka was it was
frightening to think she understood such danger.

While Alesha hadn't been in danger as such,
when her parents had locked her out of their
lives mentally she'd turned to her best friend
and her family. They'd been kind at first, but
after a few weeks her situation had begun
to pall and soon the gossip had been flying
around school about how her parents didn't
want her so why should anyone else? The first
time she'd heard that her parents couldn't face
her now that their son had died and they wished
it had been her, she'd confronted her girlfriend
and asked why she wanted to tell lies about
her. The blunt reply that she'd been speaking
the truth had gutted Alesha so much she'd hidden in her bedroom for days, denying the truth
slowly dawning on her for months. It was only
when the school rang to ask her mother why
she wasn't attending that she said she wanted
to change schools, and when that happened she

did make a few friends but never let any close enough to reveal her circumstances. Nor did her parents do anything to prove the stories untrue. That had hurt the most.

'I was thinking of you,' Kristof said, looking at her as though he were inside her head, seeing all her thoughts. 'You could get hurt in all this. There's a big heart in there.' He gently tapped her breastbone.

'I know how to look after myself.' Surely he couldn't see the hurt she'd fled from in the past. No, that was buried so deep it was invisible. Yet Alesha couldn't help wondering if he did understand that she'd been hurt because he had too. She'd like to talk to him about that, get to know a little more about what made him tick, but those weren't the rules of a fling. Certainly not theirs. So drawing in a breath, she eyeballed him. 'Are we flinging tonight?'

The surgeon face disappeared in a wide smile. 'Oh, yeah. After I've taken you to dinner at one of the best restaurants in town. Not the best in food—though it won't be a dog's dinner either—but in location. It's on the coast where you can watch the lights coming on as darkness falls and feel as if you're in a dream world. It's magic.'

Who else had he taken there in the past? The green-eyed monster raised its head and she shuddered. The thought was unbecoming of her and their fling, and took effort to banish. 'Bring it on,' she said far more cheerily than she felt. This sudden sense of being just another notch for Kristof cooled her ardour. Then reality clicked into place. She hadn't had any expectations of Kristof other than to have fun with him for a few days. He owed her nothing, as she didn't him. 'It is our last night together.'

'Yes, Alesha, it is. And what a week it's been.' His finger now caressed her jawline, his eyes unreadable, and his face reverting to professional mode. 'I'd better get back to my patients. I'll see you at the usual time.'

But he didn't rush away, hovered, that finger stilled on her chin, those eyes wary but watchful.

When Alesha was around this man her heart always thudded unusually hard. As though he could become something special. Or was already beginning to. But she had a track record of failed relationships, and this one wasn't being given the chance to become one of those. This one had a finite end date. Tonight being it. It'd be the first time she'd walk away without that sucker-punched feeling in her tummy, because she'd agreed to the terms, had wanted them. This time she'd been in control of her emotions, and hadn't fallen even halfway in love—hadn't even come close to wanting to. Yet she was going to miss Kristof more than any man she'd known. There was something genuine about him. He was loyal, had integrity, was fun. A load more things she'd appreciated, and liked in a person. Wanted, even. But more than that, she cared about him, would like to see more of him because she enjoyed his company. That wasn't love. That was too ordinary for love. Wasn't it?

With a little shake of her head, she stepped away from that beguiling touch. 'See you at six. I've got an island to visit.'

The sea was blue and she could see all the way to the bottom where tiny fish darted back and forth impervious to the boatload of tourists above them. The sky was clear and blue with not a breath of wind to jimmy up clouds. The air was hot as though they were already into full-blown summer. The coastline was beautiful, magical, and she couldn't take her eyes off the hills and brightly painted houses and the boats tied up at wharves.

She didn't want to go back to London in the morning. Back to a life without her fling partner. Except if she stayed on here Kristof wouldn't be around anyway. He was heading to London too. Different flights, different times, same destination. From now on London wasn't going to feel the same big city where she never intended putting down roots. Now there was a man living there whose company she adored. A man she'd enjoy hanging out with in their respective spare time. Not a man to get close to, or to share her fears and needs with. She'd done that in the past and had them thrown back in her face. She'd hate Kristof doing that more than anyone before, so she wasn't giving him the opportunity.

The boat nudged the wharf, bringing her out of her reveries. Time to go back to the apartment and get ready for the night ahead. The last night with Kristof, because tomorrow, despite all the thoughts whirling around her head, they were going their separate ways. The finish of their fling, of anything between them. End of getting to know each other. As she'd accepted from the beginning, and as she knew was still the right thing to do, because at the conclusion of any relationship they had she'd still wind up alone, and possibly in this case far more hurt than ever before. Best to get out while unscathed, and happy to have known Kristof without the baggage. Except a part of her still wanted to know what made him tick, what was responsible for those deep, dark looks that sometimes filled his eyes, tightened his face into serious responsibility. If she wasn't careful, she'd be wanting to help him move beyond whatever ate him up on the inside.

So, one more night. *Go, get ready and make the most of it.* Tomorrow was another day.

But as for going back to London tomorrow, where she had nothing planned to fill in the coming three weeks?

Alesha veered away from going up the hill and headed in the direction of the children's centre again to ask Antonija, 'If I stayed on for a little while would I be of use to you around here?'

'Tell me why you want to do this?'

Expecting Antonija to simply say yes, Alesha dug for a simple answer. 'If I think I could harm Capeka, then I withdraw my offer.'

Shrewd eyes studied her. 'Is this about you?'

Too shrewd. But she had a new approach to life, remember? 'I could return to London, drive through south England, hang out in cafés and bars. Or I can be useful.' She paused. 'And I believe this is the right thing for me at the moment. I need to know where I'm headed in the future.'

'Enjoy the weekend and join us on Monday.' Welcoming arms wrapped her up in a hug. 'And thank you.'

'No, thank you.'

And thank you, Kristof, for showing there are other ways to form relationships of all kinds.

Those couldn't be tears threatening. She didn't do crying.

The restaurant was intimate and stylish. Alesha looked around and felt a pang of longing. Not for the wealth that went with dining in a place like this, but for the week she'd had. Raising her glass to Kristof, she said, 'Thank you for a wonderful few days. You've really made my holiday.'

Worry rose in his face. 'Tomorrow you go back to reality. You'll be all right?'

Yes, she would, again thanks to Kristof. Maybe she should give herself a pat on the back for getting out there and not sitting around sulking in the apartment. 'Relax. I am not going to come knocking on your door in London demanding more attention. I only hope you've enjoyed these few days half as much as I have.'

His glass lifted towards her. 'I have. Thank you back. Not that it's over just yet.' His mouth softened into a smile that sent threads of warmth right down to her toes.

'Thank goodness.' She grinned back. Another night of passion to top off the week was exactly what she required. Who'd have thought on Saturday that she'd be feeling so relaxed and happy? Certainly not her. It seemed being strong and not getting involved suited her after all. 'I'm not going back to London tomorrow. I hadn't made any fixed plans to fill in the weeks other than apply for jobs through the agency, and now that's sorted with a six-month position on a paediatric ward starting in three weeks.' She grinned. 'I had a video interview with the recruitment officer at the hospital yesterday and got an email this morning saying the job is mine.'

He tapped the rim of her glass with his. 'Congratulations. You never mentioned anything about this.'

'Didn't want to jinx my chances. Anyway, I got to thinking about what I'd do for the weeks in between and suddenly it all seems ridiculous bumming around visiting places, wasting time, when I could be making myself useful.'

One black eyebrow rose. 'Next you'll be signing up for a permanent job somewhere.'

Alesha sipped her wine before nodding. 'You know what? That wouldn't be the end of the world. I've been drifting too long, looking for something to come along I might like when in fact I probably should settle and turn my life into what I want it to be. In other words,

I need to stop relying on other people to set the standard.'

The serious face was slipping into place. 'Is that why you weren't broken-hearted when Luke pulled the plug?'

'I was never in love with him, desperately or otherwise.' How embarrassing was this? Though putting it out there was like letting a heavy weight go. And letting Kristof know where she stood. 'I liked him a lot and wanted something more—to have a chance at a future together. At least I thought I did. We seemed compatible, but it could be that wasn't enough.'

'And now?' There was an edge to Kristof's question she didn't understand.

Alesha didn't rush her answer. It needed considered thought. After this week she finally understood she did want to go for the whole love package where she loved and was loved in return, but she didn't want second best. Did not want to wait for a man to condescend to love her a little bit. Not any more. Staring around the room, she sipped her wine, not really seeing anyone or anything until her gaze came back to Kristof. 'I'm ready to move on alone, to be the person I want to be without anyone else's input.' Then she'd have more to offer to the right man.

His head tilted to the side as he studied her.

Then the happy face returned and he grinned. 'Then let's finish the week with a bang. We'll take a bottle of your favourite champagne back to the apartment and sit by the pool watching the city below before I take you to your bed for one last night of pleasure.'

'I can't argue with that,' she replied, setting her glass aside. No way was she drinking too much. She wanted to remember every word, every touch, every moment. And she wanted them to be the best ever.

Three-forty. Kristof rolled towards the sleeping, warm and curvaceous body beside him and wrapped his arms around Alesha, brought her butt up against his manhood, and snuggled his face into the soft place between her shoulder blades. It had been a wonderful week. Filled with pleasure and passion, fun and laughter; no grating barbs, no nasty moments. And now it was over. Within a couple of hours he'd climb out of bed and walk up the hill to get ready to head to the airport and home.

No regrets. No ties. No demands made on him. A perfect end to a perfect week.

And yet... It wasn't as easy as it sounded. If ever there was a woman he might consider settling down with, falling in love with, Ale-

sha rang all the bells. She was beautiful inside
and out. But she wasn't ready. There were a
lot of issues holding her back. She mightn't
have talked about them but they were there
if a guy knew where to look. He'd seen a hint
of pain that first night when she'd admitted
to being set up for the holiday of a lifetime
that didn't happen. The pain that wasn't about
being dumped but about lots of other things.
Almost an acceptance because it had happened
before and she seemed to expect it to happen
again.

His lips brushed her silky skin, his nose
breathed in the scent of woman. His woman.
No, not his. Not once the sun came up. That
was not reluctance to let go churning his
gut. That was reality and practicality. Loving a woman was not on his to-do list. Even
if it happened he'd never do anything about
it. Loving people meant setting his heart up
for danger, to be sliced up piece by piece and
tossed aside. To be vulnerable again. He'd be
a damned slow learner if he let that happen.
His ex-wife had proved how right his father
had been. Love was relative to the effort someone wanted to put into it. He'd given his all to
his father, and to Cally, and got only scraps
back. His mother might've forgiven him and
still loved him fiercely, but that didn't make it

any easier to go out there and fall in love again. He carried a weight of guilt over not believing his mother would never deliberately hurt him.

But if he'd ever feel free enough to try marriage he knew he'd found the woman to take the chance with. Except he wasn't going to. The consequences could be catastrophic.

Rolling onto his back, Kristof brought Alesha with him so that she was sprawled across his chest, his belly, his rising manhood.

'Mmm…' she muttered sleepily. 'What time is it?'

'Time enough for me to make love to you again.' Make love? Or have sex? What did a name for it matter? They'd come together, share a moment, take and give pleasure. Call it what he liked, that wouldn't change the sensations, the need and the caring. This was one special lady and he was going to miss her. Far too much. But he'd get over her eventually. He had to.

'Oh, goodie.' She wriggled over so that she was facing him, her hands reaching for his shoulders, a simple touch ramping up the heat pouring through his already hot body.

Clasping her hips, he lifted her to straddle him, and lowered her over his manhood. Groaned as her moisture encompassed his throbbing need. She was always ready for him, a turn-on if he wasn't already turned on. Touching Alesha sent waves of desire rippling through her, and made her cry out. As she shuddered and gripped him he lost himself within her for one last time.

Dressed in hurriedly pulled-on shorts and shirt, Alesha hung over the parapet at the far end of the pool and watched Kristof striding up the hill as he had every day she'd been here. Confident, relaxed, ready for whatever came his way. Solid, strong, more masculine than any male had the right to be. That dark-blond hair, those wide shoulders, the long legs—only a start to the whole package.

Her heart sank further with every step he took away from her and their week. She had no right to be sad. They had agreed on a fling with a finite duration, and that was what they'd had. What she hadn't expected was the intensity of their lovemaking, or the way she'd begun to hang out for Kristof's voice at the end of the day, or how, when he was with her, she was his focus—as though he cared about her and what *she* did. She was going to miss that. Miss *him*.

But…

It was time to let go, get out in the world and make a life for herself that didn't require trying to find a compatible man who could once and for all prove to her she was lovable. So far no one had come along to love her in the only way she now accepted she needed—as in for ever, regardless of the stuff-ups she made. She'd been looking too hard, and probably chased away the men she'd known with her need for constant reassurance.

Whereas Kristof hadn't been chased away simply because they'd agreed to one week together and then to go their own ways. It had worked, despite the sadness pulling at her now.

As he disappeared around the corner at the top of the hill the sadness engulfing her grew heavier. 'Bye, Kristof.' She'd never see him again. It was how it was, and part of her was glad they wouldn't get the chance to fall out. She didn't want to be hurt by Kristof, nor to hurt him back. A bigger portion of her head, her heart, her need, wanted him to spin around and come racing down the hill to bang on the outside door leading into the complex as he yelled for her to let him back in.

It wasn't going to happen.

It was time to move on.

Starting with packing her bag and having some breakfast. Later she'd walk up the hill, following Kristof's tracks to his mother's house, and unpack her few belongings in a spare bedroom that was to be hers while she stayed on in Dubrovnik. Later, when there was no chance of bumping into Kristof. He'd made it plain when he left her bed they weren't going to see each other again, and she'd give him that. He'd done so much for her this week. And to see him one more time would be dragging out the sadness. It was time to let go. Not that she was supposed to have been caught up with him anyway. But like a great holiday, a seriously wonderful fling didn't evaporate into dusty memories within minutes.

Wrapping her arms around her waist, she smiled. It was unlikely she'd ever forget this past week. They'd made such magic memories, how could she?

Antonija welcomed her like a long-lost friend even though it was less than twenty-four hours since they'd talked about her staying on to help at the children's home. 'Here's a set of keys to my house. Come and go as you please. I've given you Kristof's room as it's got the best view.'

Kristof's room? Oh, no, that wasn't going to help with putting last week in its place. 'Thank you. I will spend most of my time down with the children though.'

'We have a busy schedule. Kristof's friend's

coming across from London for a week. He's a paediatric specialist and will see each child during his visit for general medical check-ups. I intend for you to help him. But you must get out and enjoy the city as well.'

'No problem.' Kristof's room. Kristof's friend. This woman was missing her son already. Maybe she never stopped missing him when he headed back to London. Alesha could relate to that. She was missing him too, and she hadn't spent the days in his sphere, except when she'd worked in Theatre with him that once. But those nights… 'I know you said take the weekend off but I'd prefer to see the kids today.'

'That'd be lovely. Some of them want to go to the park and an extra pair of eyes would help the staff no end.' The older woman gave a weary smile. 'The children do like to run wild a bit. It's often because of their background and being left to their own devices too much. Some of them, anyway.'

'Then they find you.' Alesha felt for this kind woman who, from what she'd seen, gave and gave of herself. 'When did you open the refuge?'

'Fifteen years ago when I returned home from London. I felt I'd had a good life and wanted to do what I could for those less fortunate. I never expected there to be so many children wanting a little love and support. That's all most of them want really. Not many are ill.'

'So the surgeons and other visiting specialists are for the general population?'

'The very poor at the end of the waiting list.'

'Right, let's get cracking.'

Alesha dropped her bag in the room that was Kristof's. Looking around, she found nothing to remind her of him. The décor was simple. No photos adorned the walls or the top of the dresser. No discarded jacket or shirt. Impersonal about described it. His idea of home with his mother? Or his mother's way of keeping her son at arm's length? That didn't explain the loneliness in the older woman's eyes. Kristof hid his feelings, though he had indicated he was not interested in a permanent relationship. Did that include one with his mother? Something had gone wrong for these two, and still Kristof came to Dubrovnik to help his mother out with her project, *and* he sought help from other qualified people for her children. Interesting.

The walk to the park with seven kids aged between eight and eleven was fun and kept Alesha on her toes the whole time. Two other staff members accompanied them, taking a soccer ball with them. The game was hilarious and no one took it seriously. Until one girl started gasping for breath. 'Marija? What's happening?'

Not understanding a word the child said had Alesha tensed up and extra vigilant as she assessed the situation. Then the man who was with them pulled an inhaler from his pocket and pushed it towards the girl, saying something that Alesha could only hope was to breathe deep with the puffer.

'Asthma?' she asked one of the staff and got a nod.

The girl was banging her chest and Alesha caught her hands and held them gently. 'Don't hurt yourself.' Her chest would be painful as the airways would've filled with mucous. Alesha took the inhaler and pressed it carefully between the girl's lips and squeezed it to express the bronchodilator into her airways to ease the tightness. 'Breathe in slowly,' which was really all the girl could manage anyway. Breathing out was a struggle. 'That's the girl.' With one hand she rubbed her back slowly, quietly. If only she spoke Croatian, this would be so much easier. Let's face it, learning Croatian wasn't on most people's to-do list.

The other children had gathered round to watch and Alesha shooed them away, administered more puffs of Ventolin. Now what? The girl was not in any condition to walk the two kilometres back to the centre, especially since the temperature was around thirty. Her breathing was not settling, giving Alesha cause for concern. When she looked to the other two adults they shrugged as if to say they didn't know what to do.

Alesha sighed. Only one thing for it. Try to walk slowly as far as possible and then piggyback the girl if she had to. She pointed to herself and the girl, then in the direction they'd come from. 'I'll take her back.'

They nodded, said something which could've been acknowledgment or an order for takeout food for all she knew.

Taking the child's hand, Alesha set out. The girl's breathing had improved marginally but she didn't feel confident Marija was up to much walking. Soon she had hauled her up on her back and was trudging the pavement along the roads back to the children's home and a general check-up with the local trainee doctor putting in some hours over the weekend. All the way she kept up a monologue about anything that came to mind. Twice she stopped to administer another puff from the inhaler.

Urgency drove her to get back to the home. Running wasn't possible. She had too much weight on her back and it was far too hot. Her brisk pace had to do.

By the time she dragged her load up the front steps of the shelter she was exhausted, and soaking in sweat, especially where the child lay sprawled across her back.

'Alesha? What's the matter?' The doctor rushed out of a front room where he must've noticed her arriving.

Thank goodness he spoke English. 'Asthma attack. At least that's what I'm presuming the problem is. I can't get it under control out in that heat.'

'Give her to me.' The young man lifted the girl away and took her straight into the treatment room.

Alesha rolled her cramped shoulders, grimacing as muscles protested, and then followed her charge. 'The inhaler we used is empty.'

The doctor said, 'There're more in the storeroom. You have a key?'

'Not yet.'

'I'll be back.'

Alesha took the girl's hand in hers. 'You'll be right soon.'

The girl blinked and tears spilled down her cheeks as she tried to force air out of her lungs. Then the doctor was back and this time the inhaler started having an effect almost immediately.

'What you did for Marija today was over and above,' Antonija told Alesha over dinner that night.

'It was fine. We had to get back and it was the only way I could think of.'

'We do have taxis in town.' Kristof's mother laughed. 'One of the others could've told the driver where to go.'

'I did look for one but guess they all had better things to do down at the Old City.' Every time she'd been down there taxis were doing a roaring trade and wouldn't be bothered with cruising the back streets where they were unlikely to get a passenger.

'Are you going out tonight?'

'I don't think so.' Funny, but she didn't have the energy. Nor the inclination. It seemed that spending most of the night making out with Kristof had used up her energy stores. Throw in carrying Marija those couple of kilometres and the idea of walking down to Port Gruž or anywhere else didn't appeal. Nor did going alone. 'I'll have an early night instead.'

On Sunday afternoon Kristof headed into his office to go through patient notes for tomorrow's surgeries. One hip replacement for a sixty-two-year-old man, and a knee replacement for a thirty-one-year-old woman. All straightforward, except the woman had a heart condition that needed a cardiologist on board in case anything went wrong in that area. He'd tried to do the knee replacement three months ago but the woman had gone into cardiac arrhythmia while being prepped for Theatre. He did not want that happening again. For one, it had stressed his patient out to the max, and for two, she desperately wanted this new knee so she could start walking and getting fit and lean again so that her heart could settle down and play nice.

Tomorrow would be a challenge, but he loved those. As long as the outcome was satisfactory. He strived for perfection, hated settling for less when his patients put so much trust in him. In Theatre, being in charge of an operation, was the place where he knew he was in control. Where he had the knowledge and skills patients needed, where he was top of his game. But… But there were the days when a body didn't do as it was supposed to, like this woman's heart. At least that had happened before he'd begun the procedure. He hadn't even arrived in the hospital. Not that he'd felt any happier. The last time he'd struck a massive problem in Theatre the patient, a youngster of seven, had haemorrhaged all over the show from an aneurism no one had seen coming.

Kristof sighed and banged his feet down on his desktop. There were days he hated his job. The days that no amount of training and knowledge and skill could do any good. Days that just turned out to be ghastly for no apparent fault of his or anyone's. It didn't stop him feeling guilty though. Picking up the woman's file, he began reading the details he knew off by heart. No such thing as taking anything for granted when her life might depend upon him.

'Welcome home. I see you're operating on Maggie Shattersgood tomorrow.'

Kristof's head flipped up and he eyeballed his mate, Harry. 'Yes. Just going over everything.'

Harry pulled out a chair and plonked his butt down. 'So how was Dubrovnik?'

'Same as usual.'

Except there was this woman who'd been special.

'No scandal, no rampaging parties? Man, you're getting dull.'

'Says the guy who goes home to his wife and three kids every night, sober as a judge.' Kristof grinned, ignoring the sense of loss that gave him. Why did he want that now? He never had before. Not even back when he and Cally were a couple had he thought they might possibly get to that stage where he'd feel comfortable enough to bring children into the world.

'Yeah, well, I kind of love it.' Harry might *sound* sheepish, but he didn't look it at all.

And I'm not jealous.

Kristof sucked his lips in. They'd certainly had some heavy nights partying in the past, way back when there had been just the two of them to think about, but they'd barely been out of nappies. Now, older, not necessarily wiser, but supposedly serious and professional, they didn't do any of that any more. 'Fill me in on the gossip. There must've been plenty happening while I've been gone.'

'How long have you got?' Harry's feet hit the other side of the desk top. 'Any beer in that fridge?'

The tiny, one-shelf cooling box. 'Yep, a couple. Pass me one while you're at it.'

Harry grunted and got back on his feet. 'So if you were being all proper and no parties what did you do when you weren't operating?'

Having unbelievable sex with an amazing Kiwi woman.

'Attended a charity dinner to raise money for the home.'

With an amazing Kiwi woman.

'Took a boat to Cavtat for dinner, visited the Old City.'

Did more than I've done in Dubrovnik in years. With an amazing...

Yeah, well. That was last week. Now he was back into his real life where surgery and patients and colleagues were the order of the day, and often a fair whack of the night.

'Alone?' Harry was studying him, but then the guy was a haematologist so studying specimens was his trade.

'Why wouldn't I be?'

'Because maybe it's time you weren't.'

Here we go again.

Only weeks before he'd left for Dubrovnik Harry and his wife had given him a speech about living alone and not finding a partner. They'd gone on and on about how he was becoming more solitary by the day. How he was turning into a serious surgeon twenty-four-seven, never letting up for fun. 'I already read that memo. It doesn't pertain to me.'

Just like that, an image of Alesha lying on the bed half covered in a sheet sprang into his head and he couldn't breathe. There was so much to like about her. So much to remember. To want to revisit. He could be in trouble here.

'Here, get this into you.' A cold, moist bottle was forced between his fingers. 'You look like you could do with something more powerful than cold H2O.'

Thanks, Harry.

Kristof lifted the bottle to his lips and drank deep of the cool, refreshing beer. Which did nothing to banish that picture from the front of his skull. She was so beautiful, so tantalising. And broken in some way.

Don't forget that. That's what will keep you away, if you choose to step back into her world for another week of passion. She was broken, he had been: they'd never make it work. If he even wanted to, which he didn't.

'Want to tell me something?' Persistence was Harry's middle name. Sometimes it was even his first name.

'I ate squid at the charity dinner.' Sitting beside Alesha, feeling at ease with all the socialite types for the first time, not feeling as though his father was breathing over his shoulder to make sure he did everything correctly so as to impress everyone. She'd been relaxed, despite telling him she wasn't used to rubbing shoulders with the wealthy. She'd charmed everyone seated at their table with her accent and her ability to laugh at herself. 'And drank champagne.'

Now that was a mistake. Harry was going to pick up on it straight away.

Yep. 'You weren't doing that alone.'

'I shared the bottle with the whole table.' He had, and ordered another so that Alesha didn't run out of her favourite drink. Though she'd been circumspect, barely touching her glass. He'd picked that was because she didn't want to do something like come on to him again in front of his mother's guests. Because while she hadn't come on to him again all evening, she'd sure responded when he'd turned the tables and kissed her.

The ringing of Harry's phone cut across his thoughts and brought him back to reality. 'You'd better get that.'

Alesha wasn't real? Wasn't warm and friendly and gorgeous?

Sure she was, but she didn't belong in this picture of him at work with his mate talking the breeze.

'Hi, Scallywag. How was it at the pool?' Harry's eyes were soft and dewy as he spoke to one of his daughters. 'You swam how far? That's amazing, you clever clogs.'

This picture of sitting with Harry having a beer just got complicated. Harry had pulled on his father cape, while *he* still sat here as the surgeon frantically denying Alesha access to his brain—and her ignoring him. He shoved to his feet. 'Time I headed home.' To his pristine apartment where everything stayed in the place he put it until he wanted it again. No shoes with six-inch heels lying around. No discarded clothing leading a trail to his bedroom. Paradise. Or so he used to think. When had that changed? Prior to or post Alesha? Or somewhere in the middle?

Harry looked up and flapped a hand at him. 'See you tomorrow,' he mouthed before returning his full attention to his daughter.

Tomorrow and the surgical list that'd keep him busy and focused, and in a zone he understood and needed.

Not a place where a certain woman interrupted his thoughts.

Not in his office while his mate sank into the love of his children excitedly talking to him and asking when he was coming home for dinner because they were starving. Yep, he'd heard all that, and just had to get away. It was too much.

It was not the lifestyle he endeavoured to get.

It was the one he'd dreamed of having if only Cally hadn't walked all over his love in hobnailed boots.

CHAPTER SEVEN

'HOLD THIS FOR ME, will you?' A doctor held out a saline bag to Alesha.

'Sure.' She took it and waited patiently while the young woman inserted a needle into the back of their little patient's hand to give the boy much-needed fluid after a severe bout of vomiting that had left him dehydrated.

On the other side of the bed the boy's father watched, his face ashen, and his eyes bleak with worry. 'I hope it wasn't the chicken he ate for lunch that's made him so sick. He started throwing up not long after and hasn't stopped since.'

It could very likely be food poisoning. Undercooked chicken was always risky. 'Was the chicken bought from a takeout place, or home-cooked?'

'I was cooking it last night for dinner when my mother phoned to ask us to go round for a meal. I turned the element off and left the pan with the lid on to cool down, and put it in the fridge when we got home.'

The doctor looked up. 'How late was that?'

The man winced as though he was about to get told off. 'About one in the morning.'

The temperature had been unusually high yesterday. 'You wouldn't have had air-conditioning running while you were out, would you?' Alesha asked and got a nod from the doctor.

'If only I had it.' The father reached for his lad's hand, wound his much larger one around it. 'Sorry, Charlie. Your dad's such a fool.'

Alesha felt for him. 'Don't say that. You made a mistake, but that doesn't make you a fool. It's just that chicken has to be cooked right through, no pinkness at all.'

'I'm still learning to cook since my wife died. She was a champ in the kitchen, could make the dullest of foods tasty. I've got a long way to go to be half as good.' The poor guy had more than enough to deal with without beating himself up over his cooking skills.

'Sounds like you're trying and that's what counts.'

The doctor had the needle in and was attaching the tubing to it that led from the bag Alesha held. 'I think your boy is going to be fine once we get some liquid into him as well as all those nutrients that come with it.'

Alesha took a quick glance at her watch. The day couldn't go any slower if it tried. She hung the bag from the steel frame and smoothed the damp curls off Charlie's forehead. 'There you go. You'll be chasing your football before you know it.'

'I'm going to run some blood tests,' the doctor said.

'I'll get the kit.' Alesha slipped around the curtain and walked the length of the children's ward to the storeroom.

'How's it going?' Cherry asked as they passed in the hall.

After five weeks Alesha already loved this job, and had been hoping the nurse she was covering for really didn't want to return at the end of her maternity leave. Though today that idea felt tiring. 'I'm looking forward to knocking off.' Half an hour to go and she'd be able to give into the exhaustion dragging at her. Never had she felt so debilitated by it. She was sounding geriatric. 'Can't wait to get home and put my feet up.' And try not to think about Kristof. Why had one week of fun together come to mean so much? It had been two months since they'd said goodbye in Dubrovnik. She should've moved on by now, not be thinking about him at all hours of the day and night. Just because he'd inadvertently made her see she needed to be strong and not let just any guy in close didn't give him the right to take over her thoughts and emotions.

'You really wore yourself out in Dubrovnik, didn't you?'

Oh, yes. That heady week with Kristof used up a lot of energy. Add in all the walking around the city she did every night after finishing work at the home. Staying on in Dubrovnik had turned out to be the right decision. Working full time with those children had made her believe she could actually settle down somewhere and become a part of a community, get a permanent job instead of taking slots all over the show. To make herself a home where she might finally integrate herself and become a part of the local picture. As much as she loved travelling it had palled in the light of what she'd done with those sad and needy children. So much she'd stayed on right up to the day before she was due to report here. And now... Well, now everything was about to change in a way she'd never foreseen.

Cherry had turned to follow her to the storeroom. 'Want to go to the pub tonight for a game of pool and a beer or two?'

'I've got to see someone tonight.' But a game

of pool was tempting. It'd be an easy option with no conflict, no arguments or disappointments, no professional façade glaring at her. And wouldn't solve a thing.

Her stomach clenched, sent a wave of nausea roaring up her throat. She held her breath, willed her body to behave. What was a bit of tiredness anyway?

But at seven that night, when Alesha finally found the address she needed and no one answered the bell she jabbed, her body all but dropped to the step. Tightening her spine, she turned and walked back the way she'd come to the bar she'd seen on the way in. The barman smirked when she ordered a cup of tea. Too bad. It was written on the blackboard.

At eight she tried the bell again with the same result. This time she couldn't fight the sagging of her knees and hit the step hard. Shuffling around, she made her butt as comfortable as possible on the concrete and clasped her knees to her chest, and waited. And waited.

'Alesha?' It was a soft question. Or was it a dream?

She blinked her eyes open. And blinked again. Kristof towered above her, concern lacing the puzzlement in those beautiful eyes.

Bang. Her heart tightened. And she knew. No doubt at all. She'd gone and fallen in love with Kristof in the space of that intense week. Not the maybe love, or a tentative, 'see how it worked out' love. Nor the *'had a great time and then goodbye'* kind. No, this was a full-on, 'involve the head, the body and the heart' love. A deal breaker.

She gasped. There was the problem. They had to make some sort of deal tonight, and she'd gone and got her side all messed up.

'What's wrong?' he asked in his professional voice.

When Kristof strolled up the road to his apartment from the parking garage, relieved another day was over and his patients were getting through post op as well as they should be, he'd been thinking how he could shuck off the clothes of his profession and pull on shorts and a casual shirt to relax with a cold one and think of nothing more difficult than what to have for dinner.

He'd been whistling under his breath, not expecting anything to change his plans as he turned towards his front door.

Then the whistle died. His feet slowed. While his eyes locked on the sleeping form sprawled across his front step.

'Alesha?' His heart skittered around in his chest. Alesha was on *his* doorstep? Why?

Something cracked open a tiny way inside him. He slammed it shut with a deep breath and pulled back into work mode. 'What's wrong?' A pebble jabbed his knee when he knelt beside her. *Please be okay.* What had brought her here? Her long eyelashes were black against her pale skin. In his chest worry stabbed hard. Alesha had to be all right. She just had to be. He couldn't imagine her any other way, did not want anything bad to have happened to her. So much for being calm about this.

'Kristof?' She lifted her head, blinked at him. Then her eyes widened. 'I fell asleep.' Her voice was thick with sleep and surprise, as if she'd forgotten why she was here.

He had *no* idea why she was here. Alesha was the last person he'd expected to find tucked up on his doorstep. Not that he was used to finding anybody here. When they'd said goodbye in Dubrovnik that had been the wrap-up they'd agreed on. The end of a wonderful week, and not even the memories, and, yes, the longing for more in the middle of the night, had been going to change a thing. Yet here she was: the woman who wouldn't get out of his head. 'Are you all right?' Standing, he held a hand out to pull her to her feet.

She rubbed her arms and stared up at him,

caution glittering out of those brown eyes. 'Why wouldn't I be?'

'How about because you're sleeping on a front step in a busy central London location? Or because you're outside my home, which I guess means you're wanting to visit.' He didn't add, *When we'd agreed not to get in touch.*

Ignoring his outstretched hand, she scrambled to her feet, then pushed back against the door, the rumpled blouse reminding him inexplicably of the night he'd found her pacing outside the apartments dressed only in a bikini and towel. As it wasn't her clothing that was the same it had to be the look of apprehension in her face that brought back that scene so clearly.

'It's good to see you. I've been wondering how you were getting on since coming back to London. Mum said you'd enjoyed your time working with her.' Now he was prattling like a teen on a hormone high. Clamping his mouth shut, he watched Alesha and waited.

'It was great. Those kids are so resilient they could teach most of us a thing or two about surviving life's hazards.' Her breasts rose and fell.

Yes, he remembered them all too well. Warm, soft, skin like satin.

Alesha continued, hopefully unaware of

where his mind had strolled. 'I need to talk to you, but I won't stay long. Promise.' Did she just begin to cross her fingers then stop?

Stay as long as you like if I can touch you, hold you close, kiss that worry away. Make another memory.

He dug into his pocket for his keys. 'Let's go inside. Feel like a beer? Sorry, I don't have any of your favourite champagne.'

'Can I have a cup of tea?' Her teeth were chattering.

Tea? Apprehension trickled down his spine. 'No problem.' He hoped. 'Come through.' He led the way to his kitchen and plugged the kettle in before snatching a bottle of beer from the fridge. 'Sure I can't tempt you with one of these?' She had enjoyed a beer on a hot evening in Dubrovnik.

Alesha shook her head as she stared around. 'Wow. This is state-of-the-art.'

'Shame it doesn't get used as much as it should.'

'You don't do swanky dinner parties, then?' There. A glimmer of that wonderful smile that always created knots in his gut.

'Afraid not.' Kristof sipped his beer before getting a mug and a teabag.

'You really do stand alone.'

It was a statement, not a question. Seemed

Alesha had seen more of what made him tick than most people ever did, and that was all in the space of a week. He must be slipping. 'I'm too busy most of the time, and when I do stop working I like to chill out without having to put my best face on.'

'Oh, boy.' She slumped, reached for a bench stool and sank onto it.

Apprehension grew, expanding and nudging aside the need for her that had begun pushing through. 'Why are you here? I'm presuming this isn't a social call to talk about the weather.'

Cool it. Don't upset her without good reason.

Alesha wouldn't be here if it wasn't necessary. Or would she? Did she want to go back on her word and continue their fling until it petered out—or became something more? Even if she did, it wasn't happening. He wasn't about to change his mind over trusting someone with his heart. Not even Alesha, as much as she intrigued him and had got under his skin.

The kettle whistled and clicked off. He poured boiling water over the teabag, his focus entirely on Alesha. Exhaustion was undoing her usually straight posture, while her hands fidgeted at her waist.

'Stop pouring,' she said in a surprisingly strong voice. 'Water's going everywhere.'

Sure was. A puddle crept towards the edge of the bench. Grabbing the cloth, he wiped it away. 'You're good at distracting me.'

Brain-slap. So not the thing to say. What if she did want to get together again?

He'd just fed into that line.

She stood up, straightened her body, and locked a steady gaze on him.

And the bottom fell out of his world. He had no idea what this was about, but he did know his life was about to change. For ever. 'Out with it.'

'I'm pregnant.'

'Really?' That was such an old line, and not what he'd expected from Alesha. Showed how little he knew her.

'Really,' she said quietly, with dignity.

'Hang on. Not so fast.' She was pregnant. *They* were having a baby. Alesha had said so. Whether it fitted in with his plans or not. What the hell was going on? He wouldn't, *couldn't*, be a parent. Kristof sank onto the stool next to the one Alesha had vacated. 'You walk in as though you belong here to tell me I'm the father of your baby? When we always used condoms.' Didn't they? He couldn't remember not using one. But they had got carried away to the point he'd known nothing but her body and the desire crashing through him.

A slow, wary nod was her reply, as she sank back down onto the stool.

'What are *your* plans for this baby?'

What little colour was in her cheeks disappeared. 'I'm keeping it. I will love it so much it won't grow up sad and lonely like me.' Her finger jabbed her thigh. 'Don't ever ask me that again. Got it?'

In spades. 'What do you want from me?' He had to start somewhere.

Her body jerked on the chair. 'To acknowledge you are the father, and to take part in his or her life.'

'That's it?' Disbelief whacked him. Pull the other one. 'It's a lot, but what about the other things? Money, somewhere to live.' His hands slapped his hips as he charged across to the window to stare out, unseeing. The breath he drew was ragged and bitter. 'What about marriage? You want me to commit to that as well?'

'No-o.' The chair crashed on the floor.

Kristof spun around to see Alesha running for the door. 'Wait.'

'What for? More insults?' Then she was tripping, sprawling across the hall carpet, her hands automatically protecting her belly. Her baby.

His baby. 'Alesha.' His knees hit the floor

with a crack. 'Alesha, I'm sorry.' He bundled her into his arms and held her tight.

She fought him. 'Let me go.'

He didn't want to. He wanted to soothe her, make her feel better. Instead he rose and steadied her on her feet. 'Don't go. Not yet.' He'd behaved appallingly. 'You came to talk to me. Let's start. I promise not to be unkind again.'

She sank against the wall, her bottom lip trembling, her eyes filled with torment he was responsible for.

His heart stopped, and he hated himself. How monstrous had he been? No, he didn't want a baby, a child, in his life. But if one was on the way he had to man up and get on with accepting his fate. It didn't mean he had to like it.

'Call me when you've had time to get used to this,' Alesha whispered, and pushed upright.

'You're not going out on the street in this condition. Come and have that tea you wanted. I'll make you a fresh one, that first one will be ruined. We'll talk if you still want to.' He'd do all in his power to get across to her he was sorry for his reaction.

'That depends.' At least she was walking in the right direction.

'On my behaviour? I get it.' She'd shocked the pants off him. A baby. No way. Not him.

'Seeing the positive test knocked me over too.' Her mood wasn't lightening. Why would it after his outburst? 'But it was positive. I am pregnant.'

Kristof switched on the kettle, for want of something to do. He was going to be a father, one job he'd never put his hand up for. The only example he'd had of that role had turned out to be false and the biggest let-down of his life. But there was no avoiding that the unforeseeable *had* happened and he was going to be a dad. In some capacity at any rate.

Where did a guy start? How did he know what to do apart from the obvious like feeding and changing sodden nappies, things he'd learned training to be a doctor, not from his family? What if this child had high expectations of him, as he'd had of his father, and he let it—her or him—down? No, that would not happen. At least not before he'd poured everything he had into making certain he was doing his best for *his* child without getting too close emotionally.

An elbow nudged him out of the way. 'I'll get that.' A small hand took the packet of teabags from his fingers. 'Otherwise I could be here all night.' Apparently she didn't want that. Couldn't blame her at all.

Which wound him up in a flash. 'Why don't

we eat and talk, and then you can stay the night instead of catching the train home afterwards since you're so tired? Sleeping past your stop late at night is not safe.'

The boiling water went into the mug without overflowing this time, but it came close. 'Because you don't really want me here. Another reason is that my morning sickness is evening sickness and I don't eat dinner at the moment.'

His protective instincts flared, cancelling the annoyance of a moment ago. 'All the more reason for you not to leave. There's a spare room with the bed made up.' He looked at her wan face and felt a squeeze in his chest for this woman he knew and yet didn't know. 'Please.'

A solitary tear leaked out of the corner of her right eye and tracked down her cheek.

Kristof caught it with his forefinger before it dripped onto her shirt. 'We'll make this work. You're not on your own.'

'No one's ever said that to me before.' Alesha coughed.

Seemed he'd opened a floodgate, such was the torrent that poured over her face now. Reaching for her, he tucked her against his body, her wet face pressed into his chest, her arms snaking around his waist to hold on tight. Stroking her back, he felt such a tenderness for Alesha it frightened him. Somehow they'd work their way through this and be there for each other in the future. Somehow. So much for remaining removed from her. Right now, she needed him, or his support, and damned if he wasn't going to oblige. Not just because it was the right thing to do, but because he couldn't not.

Run, man, run, while you still can. Get away, protect yourself.

But he couldn't. They had to sort this. A baby, for pity's sake. Him and a baby. Alesha and a baby, yes, he could see that was no problem. But him as a dad? Poor little kid.

It was going to take some accepting that he could no longer walk away from a relationship when he'd had enough without feeling he was missing out on something essential to life. A child was for ever. He or she had ended up with Kristof as a dad and that wasn't great.

What would it be like to hold his own baby? Would his heartstrings sing? Or would the fear of letting down the child outweigh the joy that Harry had often told him came with the first sight, the first touch, the first hold of your own baby?

He so wasn't ready for this. Who was?

But there was nothing for it. He had to step up to the mark. Alesha needed him and he would not let her down.

* * *

'I've never cried so much as I have these past days.' Alesha finally pulled out of Kristof's arms and picked up her cup of much-needed tea, though her hands were so shaky she was losing most of it over the rim as she crossed to the stool. Sitting down, she gripped the mug with both hands, took little sips, holding her breath after each one. Throwing up so wasn't a good look.

Kristof asked, 'Does this mean you'll be heading back to New Zealand?'

What? The whole point of telling him about the baby was so he'd have a part in his or her life. 'No, I'm not.'

'How long can you stay on in England on your visa?'

They really knew nothing about each other. 'My mother is British so I can come and go as I please. Getting work is not a legal problem.'

'We're both from multinational families, then.' Kristof was watching her as he asked, 'Won't you want to go home now to be close to your family when the baby is born?'

Close to her family? There was a joke, albeit a sour one. 'I won't be returning to New Zealand.'

A question formed in his eyes.

She hastened to avoid it. 'I like working in

some of the large hospitals in London, and lately I've been thinking of buying my own place in a small town on the edge of the city, somewhere I can make into a home and feel like I belong.'

'In other words, settle down. Did this come before you found out you were pregnant, or after?'

'While I was helping at the children's home. The work was fulfilling in a different way from what I'm used to and I got to thinking about how I never stop anywhere for long. Yes, I've been in London now for two years, but I've spent a fair proportion of that time travelling or working in hospitals in other cities. I'm a bit like a stray cat looking for somewhere to get food and warmth before moving on.'

Too much information, girl. He's starting to look scared.

Kristof sipped his beer. 'You won't be working once the baby's born.'

She needed to correct that fast. 'Not at first, no, but eventually I'll have to go back to something.' There was money in the bank thanks to her grandmother's will. More than enough to buy a small property with a tiny backyard, and to keep her and the baby fed and clothed in reasonable comfort, because one thing she'd learned from her parents, about the only thing apart from how to abandon your child, was saving and being sensible with money, so she'd invested wisely.

'I'll support you financially so don't worry about that.'

Tea had never tasted so sour. 'I don't need that from you. I've got a nest egg back in New Zealand.' Time to start arranging for it to be transferred to a local bank.

'I'd prefer you don't touch it. For now at least.'

This was crazy. She was having their baby and they were talking about money. She never talked about that. Though yes, she could see that at some stage this discussion was probably necessary, but tonight when Kristof was still getting used to the idea he was going to be a father? 'Right. I won't. For now.'

Move on. Talk about what's really biting you. If you can.

'I will look into finding you an apartment near enough so I can visit daily.'

Her heart sank. Though why, when she'd known he'd never offer for her to move in with him? That wouldn't work when he didn't seem to want involvement on a permanent basis. It was why she was here. 'Why don't you ever want to settle down?' The question was out before she'd thought it through. Now he'd send her to the underground and her train. Forget not allowing her to go home.

'Are you asking why I haven't instantly begun plans for setting up house *together*?'

Did he have to sound so appalled? 'If you think that it was my intention to get that from you then think again. These days I am as wary as you of getting too close to someone. All I want, and I've had a few days to think about this, is for our child to be able to see as much of each of us as possible, and that we both have input into their life; with the decisions about education, sports, friends, where to live.' All the things that had stopped for her when she was nine and her parents had forgotten they had a daughter.

'Exactly. Where to live. In an apartment close by, or in a semi on the outskirts of the city that'll take time to get to and from.' Kristof stepped across the kitchen to stare out at whatever was outside. His hands were jammed in his pockets, his shoulders tense, his feet slightly splayed.

'For you.'

'Yes, for me working at Harley Street and in the hospital all hours.'

'Right, this is a problem already.' She waited. Sipped some more tea. And waited. And hardened her heart. This man had got under her skin, and she might've woken up to the fact she loved him, but she was not going to allow him to knock her off her feet. She had a child to fight for. Any relationship she got into had to be sincere and loving, so that child was safe and happy. A relationship bound up with doing the right thing and not letting hearts follow their course would not provide what her child needed. And a life lived with parents who forgot more about their child than their own issues wasn't worth much.

Finally Kristof turned and leaned back against the window sill. 'I'm sorry. I know you're not a conniving woman. I know you'll only ever want the absolute best for your child.'

'Our child.'

He nodded. 'Our child. I will want the same. Just give me time.' His chest rose as he breathed in. 'I have been married. It was enough of a disaster that I never want to re-peat the experience.'

Her heart softened—only a weeny bit. She couldn't afford to let it go all mushy on her. 'Kristof, I don't believe we know each other well enough after only one week together—a week that involved more action than talking—to consider marriage.' It was true, and at the same time it was a big, bad lie. Being married to Kristof had never occurred to her before she'd found out she was pregnant, but since then, in the dark of night when she was unable to sleep, the idea nudged her. But it wasn't happening so he was safe. *They* were safe.

The relief flooding his eyes still hurt though. Presuming his response and seeing it for real— yeah, well, that stung like a swarm of bees. Only guessing about that, mind.

'She played around on me. Often. Apparently our marriage was supposed to be an open one. Shame she didn't get around to telling me or I'd never have made that walk down the aisle in the first place.'

The man was still hurting. Did he still love this selfish woman from his past? Or was it that his heart wasn't ready to let go the pain of being abused? *That* she could understand all too well. 'Why marry you in the first place?' Bad question. Now he'd think she didn't consider him worthy of being a husband. Which so wasn't true. But it was one way of keeping him at a distance, and a distance she created was something she could control when everything seemed so up in the air. The space he kept between them was never going to shrink so she was protecting her heart, right?

'The lifestyle, my career, my family name and money, and, to be fair, me. She declared she loved me in all honesty and I believed her. Our parameters were poles apart, that's all.'

That's all?

That was huge, and not something never to be discussed before that final commitment at the altar. No wonder a darkness crept into his eyes when he was tired or facing decisions he didn't like. He had history that had made him wary, solitary, and downright sad at times.

She wanted to touch him, brush away that wariness with a kiss. Or two. To wind her arms around his waist and hold him close; to show he wasn't alone.

But that would be risking her own need to stand tall and strong. She had a baby coming who would need all her love and support, should never feel abandoned as she'd been. She needed to go for another option, get this back on track and away from the deep and meaningful stuff before she got sucked in and started begging for what she couldn't have. 'So, you mentioned dinner. What were you planning on?'

His mouth tightened, then softened into a facsimile of a smile. 'Thought you got night sickness.'

'And morning, afternoon, and all times in between. I have to eat for baby's sake so I go for small helpings often.'

'Lamb chops should go well with a Kiwi.' He crossed to open the fridge. 'I can even throw a salad together. There're new spuds in the pantry. We're good to go.'

Go nowhere, she hoped. Right now that darned exhaustion was snagging her again, making her body heavy and her eyelids heavier. She slid off the stool before she fell off and went to sit on a chair by a table at a bay window, letting her chin rest on her breast-bone.

Kristof scooped Alesha off the chair and held her against his chest as he strode down to his bedroom. Her only movement was to snuggle closer, her cheek pressed against his chest. Those eyelids did not lift one iota.

While his heart brimmed with tenderness. Damn it all. This wasn't meant to happen, this protectiveness and strange sense of belonging. But that was what Ms Alesha Milligan was doing to him, unravelling all the locks and chains on his heart, and she wasn't taking it slowly.

Lying her on his bed, he pulled a light cover over her and went to turn on the bathroom light in case she woke needing it in a hurry. He wasn't sure how much control she'd have over the nausea and she hadn't been here before. Wasn't meant to ever be here.

Pregnant? Who'd have believed it? Not him. How could he have been lax in protection when so much was at stake? As a result, his life would never be the same. The routine, the security in knowing how his days would pan out—gone.

Back by the bed he watched over her, like a warrior guarding his woman and his child. The dark shadows on her cheeks did not detract from her beauty, and those long black lashes enhanced it while at the same time making her appear fragile.

That was a myth. Alesha was strong in all the right areas. She did seem to have men issues though. A chill settled on his heart. Not with him, she didn't. He would always be there for her now. They were joined together over this child. No way was he going to walk away even when the urge to run kept sneaking up on him.

Kristof kissed his fingertips and brushed the hair off Alesha's cheek. 'Sleep tight.'

Out in the kitchen he began putting lettuce in a bowl before chopping tomatoes, cucumber, avocado, and more. It was cathartic and he took no notice of what he was doing. His mind was focused on Alesha's news.

A baby. He was going to be a dad. An honest father who'd never deceive his son. He'd say the same for his wife, if he had one, but he didn't, and wouldn't.

His mother would be stoked. She'd never hidden the fact she'd like grandchildren some day, and sooner rather than later. She did not accept that he should forgo a happy family because the last attempt had gone belly up. *She* did not agree that his father should affect how he lived his life. *She* refused to acknowledge his guilt over how her love for her son had kept her shackled to her husband until her son was old enough not to need her there all the time.

Butt out, Mum. You're getting a grandchild. Be happy about that while I try to let the rest go.

Because he had to. He'd been screwed over—twice—and who put their hand up for a third crack at it? But it seemed that had happened when he was looking the other way.

Salad done, he scrubbed spuds and put them on to boil, snatching a sprig of mint from a plant growing in a pot by the back door. Waiting for the water to come to the boil, he popped the top on a beer and stood in the doorway staring out at the minuscule patio with its wooden outdoor furniture. It was his go-to place at the end of a hectic week or when he had a mess in his head that needed sorting. Like now.

This area was too small for a child wanting to play or chase a ball.

His head jerked up. So? The baby was only weeks old in the womb, had a long way to go before chasing a ball became part of the picture.

The beer was cool and moist on his dry throat. His eyes were moist as he visualised that scene of a boy running around shrieking as he chased the ball. A boy? Was that what he wanted? A son and heir? Or a little girl with her mother's sparkling eyes and sassy smile? Warmth stole into his chest, dried his eyes. A little girl who'd love her daddy and he'd love her back—so much. The dampness returned to his eyes. He wasn't supposed to be considering love. Standing out here was doing him no good. Time to put the chops on and go see if Alesha was still dead to the world or this was a catnap she'd wake from starving hungry.

The mobile phone rang as he was adding oil to the pan.

'Mr Montfort, it's Gabby from the ward. Jeremy Walbank has developed chest pain and shortness of breath. One of the registrars is with him but I thought you'd want to know.'

Mr Walbank had had bowel surgery for cancer that morning.

'On my way. Fill me in on everything now.' Kristof listened as he turned off the gas elements. 'Sounds like a pulmonary embolism. Take bloods for haematology, coagulation and biochemistry. I'll fill out the form when I get there. Give Radiology the heads up that we'll be needing imaging.'

Quickly he scrawled Alesha a note.

Sorry, got called in to see a patient. Help yourself to anything you want. I'll be back as soon as possible to continue our discussion.
　Kristof

He refrained from adding an *X* at the end, though as he drove towards the hospital he kind of wished he had put it there. It might go some way to getting back on side with Alesha. Then again, why complicate an already complicated situation? Alesha might read more into a simple penned kiss than he meant. Or she might do a runner, head for the train and the Friday-night revellers that would be on board. She'd better not leave. If she was adamant about going home later he'd drive her.

Or she might not wake up until he got home and climbed into bed beside her.

What? Why not? He could hold her, in the most innocent way, as a comfort, as support.

Oh, yeah, as if Alesha would accept that quietly. Somehow he felt cuddling was off the agenda for now, if not for ever.

That shouldn't sadden him; he should be ecstatic she wouldn't complicate things in that respect. It did, and he wasn't.

Go figure.

CHAPTER EIGHT

ALESHA WOKE AND stared around the semi dark room. 'Where am I?'

Then nausea struck and she leapt off the bed, followed the light source to what was a fully equipped bathroom. Grateful for en suite bathrooms, she sank to her knees in front of the porcelain and let her baby rule.

Her head pounded and her eyes were filled with sleep grit. Her body felt like a well-worn car tyre, and she couldn't focus on anything except feeling so bad. Looking around the room, she saw a familiar shirt on top of the laundry basket and it all tumbled back into her mind.

She was at Kristof's and they'd been discussing the baby when she'd fallen asleep. That made her look enthusiastic, didn't it? But nowadays when the need for sleep hit there was no stopping it. Unless she was at work she usually grabbed half an hour on the couch and was good to go again. At work she put matchsticks under her eyelids and carried on regardless, triple-checking everything she did.

Laying her hand on her belly, she drew up a smile. 'Hello, little one. You're being a wee bit tough on your mum, you know? I could do without all this sickness stuff. But then I suppose it's part of the deal and if it keeps you safe and comfy then I'll manage.'

Panic gripped her. What if she got what she wished for? At the cost of her baby? Pushing to her feet, she stared at her image in the mirror. 'Stay aboard, whatever you think. I love you already. Got that?'

Raising her blouse, she regarded her flat stomach. Not a hint of what lay inside. Turning side on, she changed her mind. 'A slight curve going on.' The panic backed off as fast as it had struck. 'I can't wait to meet you. Are you a girl or a boy?' If only she could be heard and understood, she'd love to feel a kick in answer to her questions.

Then her stomach groaned. Hunger was gathering strength. Kristof had mentioned chops and salad. Her mouth salivated. She had to find the kitchen. Which proved to be interesting. The apartment made the house she shared with three others look like a shoebox. There weren't many rooms but they were all very large, furnished elegantly and tastefully. It matched Kristof's professional look, not that sexy, have-fun man who only came out after everyone else had been seen to.

Not the sort of furniture for little children to climb all over.

That was Kristof's problem, not hers. So far she didn't have any furniture, not even a bed, but if she bought a place she'd have fun selecting things to make it look pretty and comfortable and *usable*. It could also be a disaster considering her lack of experience in decorating. But learning would be exciting. She'd do the baby's room first, sleep on the floor in the meantime if necessary. This settling down was sounding better by the day.

But now she had a father-in-waiting to talk to.

Except all she found was a note. And the smell of minted potatoes, which were cooked to perfection. Sitting in the hot water must've finished them off. A delicious-looking salad in the fridge made her mouth water. All that was needed was one of those chops Kristof had mentioned. Would it be rude to cook herself one? Make that two, if the growling going on in her stomach was an indicator.

Rude or not, she couldn't wait until he came home. If he came home this side of midnight.

Getting called in to a patient often meant long hours. Kristof might be in Theatre again, and even a short operation took time to prepare for, to undertake, and then hang around to see how the patient fared. The chops definitely couldn't wait a moment longer.

As Alesha slid two chops, slightly pink in the middle, onto a plate, she heard keys being dropped on the table by the front door. 'Well timed,' she called. Then hoped it was Kristof. Someone else might live here for all she knew. Someone who'd object to finding a stranger in the kitchen making a mess. She might be able to appease them with a chop.

No, her stomach growled. *I need both those.*

'Smells wonderful,' the gruff, sexy voice relieved her of that worry, but only set in motion all the other concerns about what role he'd finally decide on in the baby department. Her baby not having a father who loved and cared about him *could not* happen.

'I'll put some more on. We can start with one each.' She was acting as if she was in charge in Kristof's kitchen. Finally she was learning not to let other people dominate her. Not that this man did that.

Stay the night.

Not too much anyway.

He stood right beside her, watching as she

added more oil to the pan, swirling it as it expanded with the heat. Then he picked up one of the cooked chops and bit into it. 'You know what you're doing.'

'Hey, I need that.' She grabbed the other before he could lay claim to it.

Kristof nodded. 'Salad and spuds after the protein?'

Alesha waved her chop between them. 'Only because I don't trust you not to steal this when I'm spooning salad onto my plate.' Was he in a good mood? Or still in shock? That raw denial seemed to have disappeared from his eyes, but she couldn't read what had replaced it.

'Come on, now. Would I do that?'

'Yes. You stole two of my deep-fried squid at the charity dinner.'

'I made up for it later.'

With the most amazing sex she'd ever experienced. Yep, she got it. Making light of a grave situation must be Kristof's way of coping. She backed away, sank onto a chair. 'We're not having sex tonight, not any night. The fling is over.'

'You're right.' Not even a hint of a smile now.

Kristof filled his plate with salad and sat down beside her at the small table. 'We did get on well when we didn't overthink things.'

Yes, but they hadn't had a baby in the picture then. The tomato was surprisingly sweet on her tongue, giving her hope other things could be too. 'Let's try to keep it that way. There's a lot at stake.'

'I agree.' His eyes were thoughtful. 'Have you told anyone else?'

She tried for a smile, but exhaustion got in the way. 'No. You had to be the first person who knew.'

'Thank you. That's important to me.'

Because she put him first? About to slip one finger across the back of his hand, she hesitated. Best not. 'I won't ever deliberately hurt you, or abuse your trust in me.'

His chair legs squeaked as they were pushed across the tiles. 'You don't know me well enough to trust me with something as important as your baby's future.'

Alesha drew herself up and locked her eyes on his. 'There are a lot of things I haven't a clue about when it comes to you, but I do know in here—' she tapped her chest '—that I can trust you to be considerate and to care about me in regards to our child. Actually, make that I trust you totally.' She really did. There were no grounds for this, and while every man she'd spent more than a couple of dates with had hurt her in one way or another this beggared belief. But she did believe it. Kristof would not do the dirty on her. How often had he watched out for her during their fling week? Attended her needs before his? That had been wonderful, worth gold.

Now she just had to prevent her heart thinking it was winning and that she was about to throw herself at Kristof. Because trust was well and good, but it wasn't the whole picture. Discovering she loved him didn't mean he reciprocated; didn't allow her to stop fighting for what her baby needed; wouldn't make the coming months a breeze to get through. Only if they could find common ground, fall in love together, make a real go of being a family.

In your dreams. Alesha.

His head came down, close to her, then his lips caressed her forehead. Inside, her temperature rose and her muscles softened, her stomach turned to goo. This was beautiful. It made her feel special. Which it shouldn't. She should back away now. Before he told her he wasn't interested in her or their baby.

Kristof beat her to it, pulling away and picking up their plates to take them to the sink. 'It's getting late. Tomorrow's Saturday. I think we should postpone further discussions until then. Go out for breakfast at the market and start making some plans.'

He expected her to stay when she hadn't agreed to. 'What time shall I meet you there?'

'Don't do that,' he growled. 'You're pushing me away.'

Was she pushing him away? If standing up for herself and showing she wouldn't be told what to do meant that then, yes, she was. 'I'm looking out for myself.'

'I get it, but staying here isn't going to prevent you doing that, and it makes sense not to go home on a train loaded with drunks and who knows what else. You'd only have to return in a few hours, hours that could be spent catching up on sleep you so desperately need if those shadows darkening your cheeks are any indication.'

'Fine. I'll stay.' What else could she say when her blood was humming with gratitude and something she'd rather not identify? Her head *was* nodding with fatigue and her legs really didn't have the strength to walk to the nearest station. 'Which bedroom shall I use?'

'Mine. It's got a bathroom within dashing distance.' His smile was strained, as if reality was finally catching up in a hurry.

All she could hope for was that she didn't wake up on the front step with a note attached telling her to go away, that he wasn't interested in becoming a parent. But he wouldn't.

She trusted him. If that made her an idiot, then sorry, but once she'd allowed him in it seemed there wasn't any way he was leaving. 'Goodnight, Kristof.'

He had his phone out. Finding out how his patient was? Or was there a significant other person in his life? She'd never asked, believing he wouldn't have had that fling if there was. 'Goodnight, Alesha.'

'Is there someone special in your life you have to tell about the baby?' She couldn't help the squeak that accompanied her question, the need to hear him say no suddenly important.

'I'm single, without anyone regular in my life. In fact you've been the only woman I've been intimate with in months.'

Good. She wouldn't ask why. That'd be pushing too hard. 'Goodnight, Kristof.' She headed down the hall, a spring in her heavy footsteps.

They were definitely like two people who'd had a hot fling and moved on to become— what?—friends with a baby on the way? Friends was good, but nowhere near enough. Though until they'd worked their way through the issues surrounding baby then it could be that friendship was the way to go. Also, far better than fighting one another every step.

Down, disappointment, down.

This was what she'd come for, before she'd realised she loved the man.

Slipping out of her blouse and skirt, Alesha slid under the sheet in her underwear. It probably wasn't wise but it was all she had, and anyway she was as well dressed as the night she'd first met Kristof. Since then he'd seen it all. Smiling, she closed her eyes and instantly fell into a deep sleep where dreams of what they'd done together, followed by other dreams of what they could do next, skidded through her night.

Kristof stood in the doorway of his bedroom watching the gentle rise and fall of the sheet covering Alesha's breasts. He wasn't leering or even thinking sexy thoughts. No, his head was full of images of her holding their baby, of crooning to a crying little one, of kissing his or her forehead and pressing him or her to her swollen breast for milk. Don't ask him how, but he believed she was going to make an excellent mother.

As for him? An excellent father? Yes, he could be, would be, as long as he didn't get it all wrong. The child had better be strong, and depend more on his—or her—mother than him. Just in case Kristof made poor judgements and hurt them all. He'd misread his father, and blamed his mother for leaving them when she'd been struggling with Dad's infidelities. If only he'd known about those before he'd shouted at her, 'If you leave I never want to see you again.' He'd believed his father to be nigh on perfect, had never once considered the man he tried to emulate might be the one transgressing the marriage boundaries. Not that he'd been able to picture his mother having an affair either. His mother had been quick to brush away his apologies when he'd learned about the mistresses but it had been too late. He'd said those awful words and there was no taking them back. She'd returned to her home town of Dubrovnik before his father had died, and he'd missed her so much, but male pride had got in the way and kept him firmly in London, until he'd finally gone to apologise, and they'd slowly started to rebuild their relationship.

Then there was his marriage. Cally had wanted for ever with him, just not only him.

He'd never hurt a woman like that, or his child, but he'd also never risk his heart again.

One week was all it had taken to turn his world around, to change his direction for ever. Was he happy about it? Honestly? No. But there was no undoing what had happened. Alesha certainly had found the right man to accidentally get pregnant with. He'd stick by her throughout and beyond, as a friend, as the father of her child.

Kristof spun away to head to his TV room. A mindless programme would help quieten the questions and let him relax enough to fall asleep. The answers were there, under lock and key, waiting for a time he was able to look at them. He wanted to believe he'd get this right. He really, really did.

Because if he was lucky enough for his child to adore him he didn't want to crack his son's world wide open to disbelief and pain; to the acknowledgment his father had made a mockery of everything he'd been raised to believe.

As *his* father had done. Had his dad gone and died quietly and with dignity? Hell, no. A massive heart attack while in his mistress's bed had been the final chapter in what had turned out to be a double life right from the day he'd married Kristof's mother and been unfaithful with the bridesmaid.

At least according to the gossip and stories at the funeral and for months afterwards.

TV wasn't distracting him.

A brandy might. But he had to be ready to return to the hospital if called.

So checking out the property market in central London was an option.

Alesha didn't want to live in the city with her baby.

There had to be give and take. Alesha had to understand he wanted to be near but that he couldn't live too far from the hospital.

Another option would be to keep this apartment and buy a larger house where she wanted and go stay there at the weekends.

Just like your father.

He wasn't having a mistress in the city and Alesha waiting for him somewhere else. That wasn't the idea. Anyway, he and Alesha weren't a couple.

Just as well he wasn't on call tomorrow. He'd be next to useless.

A light knock on the bedroom door warned Alesha she was no longer alone. 'Hello?'

'Will a cup of tea make waking up easier?' Kristof stood in the doorway, that thick dark-blond hair with a very slept-in look and a line of stubble highlighting his jawline.

Her tongue roved over her lips at the gorgeous sight. Until her stomach warned her there were more important considerations right now. Gulp. 'Excuse me.' The bathroom door slammed behind her. This was not something she wanted to share with Kristof. That was going too far. She preferred he remembered her looking half decent at least.

The man didn't take the hint. Or was too thick to understand. The door opened and he was there, holding her hair away from her face, rubbing her back, and, when it was over, handing her a warm, moist face cloth.

While her stomach cringed at Kristof seeing her like this, there was no denying the tenderness flowing through her at his kindness and concern.

'Here.' He held out a thick white robe. 'Far too large, I know, but you look cold.'

Dressed in bra and knickers, she certainly wasn't overdressed. 'Thanks.' The soft fabric smelt of Kristof as she snuggled into the garment. She blinked rapidly to banish the sudden tears. All these tears. Pregnancy seemed to mess with her hormones quite a bit.

But when was the last time anyone had done something so ordinary and yet so endearing for her? No answer came to mind, unless she went back to when she was seven and her mother cuddled her after falling off a horse. Mum.

Don't go there.

But what would her mother say about the baby?

Forget it.

Her parents had had no time for her after

Ryan got sick; they weren't going to find any for a grandchild. Especially since they were on the other side of the world. Her heart sank. It was so unfair. She was used to the abandoned feeling she'd known from the day her brother was diagnosed with acute leukaemia catching at her in unexpected moments, but it never got any easier. The sense that her parents should want to see her, talk to her, know what she was up to would not go away permanently. Sometimes that made her angry, mostly it made her sad.

'Ready to try that tea?' Kristof asked.

She nodded, her gaze lingering on him. His size filled the bathroom, his presence stole the air and her sense of gravity, made her head swirl. This man was the father of her baby. Unbelievable really, that he'd been keen enough to make love to her every night for a whole week and then welcome her into his home here in London when they weren't supposed to see each other again. A soft breath trickled over her lips. If only he could see her as a woman to spend his future with. If only she hadn't gone and fallen in love with him.

A steady hand took her elbow, and she was led out to the bedroom. 'Get back into bed until you're feeling one hundred per cent again. I'll bring your tea here.'

'I should be all right now. One bout at a time seems to be how it plays out for me.'

'Bed. Now.' There was a thread of command in his husky voice.

Alesha obeyed. She was quite liking having someone in charge for a few minutes. It gave her time to get her strength back and stop thinking about Kristof as anything other than the father of her child.

His head appeared around the door. 'Are you ready for a piece of toast? Dry or buttered?'

She shook her head. 'Just the tea. I'll eat when we get to the market.'

'You still want to go?'

Yes, she wanted to have that talk about how they were going to deal with being joint parents in separate homes, and it would be easier on her to do that away from this opulent apartment that needed knocking into comfortable, used shape. The atmosphere intimidated her at moments when she relaxed too far. She could not imagine a small child crawling around the place getting slobber on the carpet or a chair leg. 'I adore markets.'

One dark eyebrow arched and his mouth twitched. 'Should I hire a trailer for the morning's shopping?'

'A very large one.'

'You a shopaholic by any chance?' The question was laden.

'Nope. I like browsing and daydreaming but I don't usually buy up large.' Though there was a baby growing in her tummy. 'Though I might be tempted to get a teddy bear today.'

'Alesha.' The laughter had gone from his voice. 'Don't rush it. You're only a few weeks pregnant.'

Her skin tightened. 'You think I'm tempting fate?'

'I'm being super-cautious.'

'You're frightening me, is what you're doing.'

Immediately he was beside the bed, reaching for her hand to squeeze it gently. 'Sorry. I don't mean to.'

'Then why did you? Do you always look for the bad in things?'

Her hand fell from his as he stepped back. 'I'll make that tea.'

'Why are you avoiding my question?'

'I'm trying to come up with an answer.'

Looking back to their nights in Dubrovnik, she realised there'd been other times when he had changed the subject if she'd asked something personal. Oh, he'd have answers all right, just not ones he wanted to share. Great. Worked well for a relationship even of the kind they were planning—*not*. 'I would like to learn more about you.'

But he'd gone. Alesha huffed as she sat on the bed and leaned back against the headboard. Bet it took longer than usual to make the tea. Kristof wouldn't be in a hurry to talk to her now.

'So much for breakfast,' Kristof commented when they got to the market. The place was humming and the food cart had a queue to Africa. He'd thought the cooler weather might've kept people indoors, but apparently not. 'I should've made you something at home.' But then he'd have had to face up to some of Alesha's questions. She might've only asked one that morning, but answer it and there'd be more.

'I'm going to the bread stall to get something. I'm starving,' she told him. 'Then I'm grabbing a coffee. What about you?'

'Suits me perfectly. You meant to drink coffee?'

A look of annoyance lashed him. 'Okay, tea. You can't avoid talking about our baby just because we're not sitting down to breakfast. We've got all day.'

He winced. 'Actually we haven't. I've got a wedding to attend this afternoon.'

Rocking back on her heels, Alesha glared at him. 'Thanks for telling me.'

'I didn't see the need. We've got a few hours this morning.'

'Really?' She shoved the sleeve of her thick jacket up and held her wrist in front of him so he could read the time.

Another wince. Not hours, barely an hour before he had to get home to spruce himself up. 'Right, food first. We'll take it and the coffee over to one of the park benches.'

She didn't move. 'Are you trying to get out of this discussion by any chance?' One hand gripped a hip.

A hip he remembered kissing all too well. Which was totally inappropriate right now, and clouded the issue between them. 'No, but the morning did get away on us.'

With you being sick and me taking my time making your cup of tea so you might forget what you'd asked.

'Alesha, I understand you want to know where we're at and what the way forward might be.'

She did a funny twisty thing with her head as she continued that stare. 'Good. Then let's get down to it—while we're munching on food.'

'Surrounded by crowds and having to shout

to be heard?' He shook his head before taking her elbow and leading her to the bread stall. 'What would you like?'

'Two chocolate croissants.'

Hardly healthy food for junior, but he daredn't comment, merely ordered said croissants and a bacon butty for himself. At the stall next door he got a long black and a tea before they walked across to a bench, only to lose it when they were yards away. 'Blast.'

Alesha placed her tea on the path between her feet and began devouring a croissant, chocolate smearing across her upper lip.

He itched to wipe it away with his finger, or, better yet, lick it up. Instead he bit into his butty and chewed and chewed. Bacon was his favourite morning kick-start, but nothing was happening today. Sipping the over-hot coffee added to his woes when it burned his tongue. 'At least we can be thankful you don't have to return to New Zealand.'

There was that despairing look again. 'We covered this last night.'

Just kicking off the talk. 'Are you sure you're happy settling down in England? I mean, why don't you want to go home to have your baby?' It was imperative he knew. Suddenly he couldn't imagine what it would be like if she did up sticks and return home, where she must have some friends, if not family. Not to have Alesha near was beginning to worry him. And this wasn't about the baby. This was a leftover from their time in Croatia. Or was it? He didn't know. Didn't understand a thing that had happened, or been said, since those words had spilled out between them.

I'm pregnant.

'The baby's father lives in England.' The reply was too quick, as if she didn't want to say anything about what or who was—or wasn't—back in New Zealand. 'Are you afraid I'll take the baby away from you?' Now there was concern—*for him*—in her eyes.

He preferred the despair. 'I'd like you to be happy with where you are, secure in the knowledge you're doing the right thing by you and the baby.' Could he ask about her family without upsetting her too much? He would have to know some time.

'If I go south you'll take visiting rights twice a year. Fly in for a few days, have a great time at the amusement park with your child, and fly out again.' Despite the tartness in her voice that concern was still there; growing even.

He had to stop it, which meant not asking the big questions—yet. 'I want the best for you both. That's all.'

'Who hurt you, Kristof? Not your mother, surely? She worships the ground you walk on.'

You're right. She didn't.

But she was right about one thing. 'I hurt her.' Too much information. In his haste to stop this conversation he'd added fuel to the fire.

'That explains it.' Alesha was nodding as she bit into her second croissant.

Now he was in for it, if he didn't stop her in her tracks. 'Let's go look for that teddy bear.'

She sagged forward. 'I've got a better idea. Why don't you head home and get yourself ready for the wedding and I'll do my own thing?'

'Alesha, I'm...'

'You know what? I don't care what you're about to say. We'll have this conversation when you've had time to think about what you really want and in the meantime I'll get on with preparing for motherhood.' Hurt dripped off every word. The paper cup of tea spilled across the path as she turned to throw the remains of her food in the nearby bin. 'See you another time.' Her back was tight as she stalked away.

Kristof ached for her, but his feet were glued to the path. He'd achieved diversion—and hated himself for it. But telling her the truth about his sorry background and how he'd hurt his mother by believing his father? It was never going to happen. He never talked about that to anybody, and wasn't about to start.

So best he did what he was told and go get ready for his friend's wedding, *his* day of happiness.

His eyes were fixed on the back of Alesha's head as she pushed through the crowd. Admiration for her standing up to him grew. She was a fighter, in her own way. By walking away she'd handed the ball back to him. What better woman could his child have for a mother? None that he could think of. But then his thinking was all askew since he'd met her, so what did he know?

Only that she was better off without him in her life, and now he had to remain on the outside looking in, supporting her without touching her in any way, shape or form. He hadn't taken up the opportunity of having affairs when Cally had revealed hers, but what if he had his father's genes, those ones in particular? Even the best marriages had times when they didn't run smoothly. Was that when he'd show his true colours?

CHAPTER NINE

ALESHA THOUGHT ABOUT that week in Dubrovnik, how it had started out so badly and finished on a high. Her sigh was bitter sweet. If Luke had gone with her as planned her life would be so different right now. There wouldn't be a baby on the way. Love wouldn't be contracting her heart. She'd never have spent time at the Croatian children's home and found she was ready to settle down instead of planning her next trip for when this current contract ended.

'The bedrooms are small but there's lots of light,' the estate agent told her. 'And there's a little yard at the back with a patio where you could grow a few shrubs.'

The house did nothing for her. Neither had the previous two she'd seen. 'I'm sorry.' A backyard in New Zealand was huge compared to this postage-stamp-sized one.

You don't live there any more.

How true.

'Well, I don't have any more properties to show you at the moment.' The woman strode through the house. 'You might have to re-think your prerequisites or come up with more money to get what you want.'

Best to sort out other things first. 'I'll think about those options.' The woman wasn't overly friendly, not like the two sales people she'd been out with during the previous few days. They hadn't given up on her yet, had more viewings for next week. 'Thank you very much for showing me these houses.'

'She doesn't believe I can afford a property,' Alesha told Kristof over the phone that evening when they connected for a chat as they'd done every couple of nights since their disagreement in the market over two weeks ago.

'Didn't she ask you pertinent questions before taking you viewing?' Kristof's voice was always warm and sexy over the phone, almost as if their disagreement hadn't happened, and reminding her of what she couldn't have. If only she could see his face, his eyes.

No wonder she got little sleep at night. Kristof's voice was always there, reminding her of the boat ride to Cavtat, the charity dinner where she'd bought those vouchers, the walk around the Old City, and the lovemaking—

sorry, sex—in her snazzy little apartment. Exhaustion had become a part of her day, and baby wasn't responsible for all of it.

'I filled out a fair amount of paperwork, yes. But a part of me thinks I'm being negative without trying.'

'You might not be ready to make a decision like this.' He drew a breath. 'You can stay with me when you stop work if that'll give you breathing space while you make up your mind. Or I can buy that apartment around the corner from here. If it doesn't work out it will still give you time to come up with an alternative.'

Then she'd be beholden to him. Buying an apartment in high-end London wasn't exactly like getting the fish that was on special for dinner. Or maybe it was for Kristof. How wealthy was he? His home, clothes, his car, all spoke of money, but what would she know coming from her background where clothes came from chain stores? As for cars and houses, she didn't know what her parents had now. When the world tipped upside down because of Ryan's illness the car had been an average family wagon, and the house middle class newish in Christchurch. She'd gone to see it before leaving for England but it'd been wrecked in the earthquake and bowled over by bulldozers.

Seemingly, her parents had walked away with the insurance pay-out in their pockets.

'Alesha?'

'That's a lovely offer but I'll keep looking.'

'You pushing me away again?'

'No. Again.' Or was she? 'Kristof, can we take things one at a time? The house issue is not urgent...'

'Do you understand how long it can take for a purchase to go through?' he interrupted.

'Anything from a few days to a few weeks.'

'That might be the case where you come from, but not here. There are months involved with this.'

'Up the pressure, why don't you?' But she should've thought to ask about that. Showed how mixed up her brain was these days. 'About taking things one at a time, I'm having a scan tomorrow.'

'I've got surgery.'

He hadn't asked what time her appointment was. 'I see.' She really did. The blinkers had been lifting, now they were wide open. For all his offers of help regarding most things to do with the baby, he did not want to be a part of the pregnancy. So he was going to remain remote when it came to interacting with the baby. Her heart broke for their child. She knew all too well what that felt like, the hurt and bewilderment that followed her through life, the questions about what she'd done to earn the brush-off. Wasn't she good enough? For them? Her baby would not know that. Would not. Her heart also snapped for herself. They were not going to become a 'couple'.

'Kristof,' she snapped. Then swallowed and took a calming breath, though it went nowhere near to slowing her angry pulse rate. 'Are you sure you do not want to see your baby for the first time at the scan? Are you telling me this doesn't matter to you at all?'

Silence. Long and awkward.

She waited, holding her breath. Then had to draw in air, and wait again. In the end she said, 'Think about it. Goodnight, Kristof,' and hung up.

Gutted. That was how she felt. Hollowed out and stomped on. The man she loved was dodging the important issues involving his child. Every parent she knew had said that first scan was exciting beyond description. Even a man with commitment issues would want to be there. Wouldn't he? It was why she'd mentioned the appointment, not wanting to have him feel he was missing out. She'd got that wrong, hadn't she? It wasn't as though she'd been asking for something for herself.

'Why?' she cried as tears streamed down

her cheeks. She hadn't asked for a marriage proposal or the signing over of all Kristof's assets into the baby's name. Only involvement.

Her phone rang. 'Kristof' flicked up on the screen.

This had better be good. 'Yes?'

'What time?'

'Five-thirty.' She gave the name of the hospital.

'I'll be there.'

'I'm glad. For your sake.' She wasn't saying it would be nice to have him with her for this important appointment. He'd pull out. Instead he had to do it for himself and the baby.

Alesha ended the call and stared at the mess on the kitchen bench. Everyone had left in a hurry that morning, leaving dishes and empty bread bags lying around. For once she didn't care.

She'd done it. Kristof was coming. Because she'd pricked his conscience? Or because he'd taken a minute to rethink his instant refusal? It didn't matter. She'd stuck up for her baby. She, who spent most of her life trying to please people rather than create waves, had put her baby before her own needs. While having Kristof there during the scan would help her, it was the baby she needed to be able to tell later 'when your father and I first saw you', not have to dodge the question of why Dad wasn't there.

Kristof was late through no fault of his own. 'I'm five minutes away.'

'I'll try to get the radiology tech to hold off, but she's wanting to finish for the day.' Alesha sounded peeved, as well she might.

But welcome to his world where patients came first, and often second and third. Often? Always. Things were going to have to change if he took this fathering thing seriously. Why wouldn't he? He was not going to be *his* father. No kid deserved that.

So you're going to buy a house outside the city and ask Alesha to marry you so you can all play happy families?

He tripped up the steps leading into the unit. Trying to do the right thing by the baby and Alesha was impossible when they were at odds. The baby needed all he could provide without him getting close; Alesha did not need him as a husband who was only there to provide the basics. He wasn't marrying without involving his heart. Back to the beginning. Full circle. No marriage. His mouth dried, and his heart slowed.

'Hi, you made it.' She was waiting outside

the entrance to Radiology, relief beaming out of those beautiful eyes.

And drilling into his gut. Reminding him of how well they fitted together. Not only physically, but also they seemed to agree on the most important things. Suddenly the stress of getting here, of even having to be here, fell away and he reached for her hand. 'Let's go do this.' He wanted the first glimpse of his son or daughter more than anything.

Her fingers slipped between his; warm, soft, Alesha.

'Now, there's a surprise.' The girl pushing her scanner into Alesha's stomach grinned. 'There are two in there.'

'What?' The word exploded out of Kristof. 'Twins?'

'Two?' squeaked a stunned Alesha. 'Two babies. Oh, my.'

The girl nodded as she studied the screen in front of her. 'That explains your exhaustion, I'd say.'

Alesha murmured, 'Are you sure?'

Kristof wrapped an arm over her shoulders, held her tight. This was colossal. One baby in their situation was big, but two? They had a lot to consider. Not that anything had really changed. 'Do we know what we're getting?'

'Do you want to?' The girl looked from him to Alesha.

Alesha nibbled her bottom lip. 'I think I do. When it was only one baby I thought I'd like to be surprised, but two? I want to know.'

The scanner pushed against her belly and the images on the screen showed two tiny figures. 'How can you tell whether they're boys or girls?' Kristof asked. A dumb question. The woman was well qualified for this, but right now that picture seemed fuzzy to him and those babies so tiny they blurred before his eyes. He rubbed them and his hand came away damp. He was crying? Hadn't done that since he was a kid. He slashed harder at his face. It didn't do to be seen sniffling.

Alesha had no problems with crying. Buckets were needed to collect her tears. The tissues the girl passed her were quickly turned into a sodden ball and another box had to be found. Then she turned into him, buried her face against his shoulder, and saturated his shirt as well.

A boy *and* a girl. It was as though fate had caught him out and was playing a full hand in case it didn't get another chance. His lungs weren't coping. His heart had lost the ability to do slow and steady. Those images told him what Alesha hadn't been able to, what he hadn't been able to grasp fully. 'I'm going to be a dad.' As in raise, mentor, play with, cherish for ever, those babies. *Love* them regardless. 'Want to share those tissues?'

'I might have to agree to that apartment around the corner,' Alesha told Kristof over a cup of tea back at his place. 'Two babies are going to be a handful and if you're close by that'd help.'

'We'll get a nanny.'

Oh, Kristof. 'No, we won't. I am going to bring up my children. I will not leave them in someone else's care.' All the angst over being abandoned roared up through her and she was on her feet staring into Kristof's startled eyes. 'Never.'

'Whoa. Take it easy. I was only trying to make things better, not worse.' He sank onto a kitchen stool so he was at her level when she returned to her seat.

'Well, you weren't. Never, ever, suggest that again. You hear?'

'I think the whole street heard.' Then his lips flattened. 'Sorry. Not the right time for flippancy. But I'm out of my depth here. What do you want?'

He was trying to help. She had to drop the anger. It wasn't his fault her parents did what they did. 'My turn to apologise.' She retreated to her stool and tried to pick up her cup without sloshing tea everywhere. That was a fail.

'Talk to me, Alesha. How are you going to manage? Financially, for one. Raise two children while working, for another. There's something more going on here that I have no clue about.'

'I have my grandmother's money. She died when I was eleven and I couldn't touch the money till I was twenty-one. The lawyer she appointed invested very wisely for me.'

'There's more to this. Someone's hurt you, haven't they?'

As if he told her things about his past? But they'd get nowhere if they both kept this up. One of them had to start letting go and revealing what made them tick. It wouldn't be Kristof. He was too tight, too removed once the fun stopped. But could she talk to him about her family? Could she not? Her babies were depending on her getting things sorted before they arrived. Sorted properly, not doing a shoddy job that they'd all live to regret.

This time the tea didn't go over the edge of the mug when she picked it up, though it was now lukewarm. Guess she couldn't have it all. Sipping, she hoped her stomach didn't choose now to make a nuisance of itself. 'My brother died of AML when I was ten.' She hesitated.

Took another sip. 'It was horrible. My parents couldn't deal with it.' She blinked, stared all around the room but not at Kristof. If his eyes filled with sympathy she'd fall apart.

His hand covered her one on her thigh. He didn't say a word. She still nearly fell to shreds.

More tea, more deep breathing. Then, 'They were lost in their grief, and I—from the day Ryan's bone-marrow result was delivered I didn't have parents any more. Not ones who were there for me. I was nine.'

'Who took care of you?'

'I did. I ate when I was hungry, shopped with the money Dad left lying around when the cupboards were bare, attended school to get away from the gloom pervading our house. I didn't go without, but it wasn't fun either.' No one asking how did school go, or questioning why she wanted to change schools. No acknowledgment she existed.

No love.

She could've handled everything else if her parents had only shown her half what they gave Ryan, even after he died.

Were those swear words spilling from Kristof's mouth? For her?

Finally Alesha looked at him. A mix of anger and sorrow twisted his mouth, darkened his eyes. He leaned closer, both hands held out to her.

It would be so simple to lean in against him and let go of her own anger and disappointment, let Kristof take charge. Too easy. Because ultimately she had to be strong for herself, and those babies. Leaping up, she paced across the room, back and forth, back and forth.

'Alesha, go easy. Let me help you. Now, and later with the babies.'

Babies. Not one, but two. She'd thought it would be hard raising one, now there was another one to think of. Could she do this?

She had to. *Wanted to.* But now she was afraid. Double trouble was what people said of twins. Double worry that she'd get it right. Twins. 'Are there twins in your family?' As far as she was aware there weren't any in her family.

'I don't recall any. Guess we managed them all by ourselves.' His light tone was forced, as though trying to pacify her.

It wasn't working. The agitation churning her insides got faster, harder, meaner. She had to get out of here. 'I'm going home.' Slinging her bag over her shoulder, she headed for the front door. Until her stomach warned it had other ideas. A quick detour took her to the bathroom.

* * *

Kristof left Alesha alone, knowing full well he was not welcome this time. But he was biting to get in there and hold her. Except no amount of caressing or soothing was going to work. Her story about her family appalled him. They'd done a lot of damage to Alesha, back when she was a child, and again tonight as she'd laid out the bare basics.

He was furious for her. How could parents do that to their daughter? Grief could paralyse a person, but to cast their child adrift? When she was so young? Actually, it didn't matter what age she was; it was wrong, and horrid, and totally incomprehensible. No wonder she never talked about her past.

Ten minutes ticked by. He couldn't stand waiting any longer. A light tap on the bathroom door and he let himself in. His heart hit his boots.

Alesha looked so forlorn he felt as though he'd been slapped by a raging elephant. Having lowered the lid of the toilet she sat huddled with her arms around her knees, drowning in tears. Silent ones streaming all over her face and onto her arms.

She didn't raise her head when he said, 'You are going to be the best mother ever.'

Not a movement, not a whimper. Just those blasted tears.

Kristof sank down onto his haunches beside her and held the tissue box at the ready. How he hated tears. He didn't know what to do about them. How to stop them. How to obliterate the pain that caused them. He was useless. He waited some more.

Until a shaky hand reached for the box and tugged out a handful of tissues.

He watched as Alesha began mopping up her face, her chin, the backs of her arms. He handed her more tissues and removed the sodden ball from her hand.

She yawned. Her eyes were swollen and dull, exhaustion drew at her cheeks. Another yawn made up his mind.

'Come on. You're going to bed.' Leaning down, he lifted her into his arms, ready to put her down gently if she tried to get away.

Instead she snuggled into him, surprising the breath out of his body. Hope soared. She'd turned to him, not away. They might be able to work something out where Alesha had all the help she needed and he was there in the background to look out for her and the babies. She was right. Everything had got harder now that there were twins on the way. Solo parenting, even with him there for her, was hard, and that was with one child.

In his bedroom he toed the bedcover aside and laid Alesha down.

Another of those enormous yawns pulled at her.

Pulling the cover up to her chin, he kissed her hot cheeks. 'Get some sleep.'

Her hand snatched his. 'Twins. It's too much. I won't cope.'

'It's okay. *We'll* cope.'

Shuffling up the bed, she leant back against his headboard. 'No. *I* have to. I have to fight for my children. I can't fall apart when the going gets rough. I have to fight for them, no matter what tries to knock me off course.'

'You don't think you're already doing that?' He parked his butt on the edge of the bed and reached for her hands again.

'I don't know.' She pulled them away and tucked them on her stomach under the cover. 'Maybe I should go home.'

'You want to ride a train now?' What was wrong with staying here with him for the night? Disappointment slayed him.

'Back to New Zealand.'

Forget being disappointed. Try shocked.

Hadn't she been adamant there was nothing for her back there? 'Why?'

'Smaller city, a health system I understand.'

'No family or friends to support you. No father of the babies you're going to have there to take his turn at feeding and changing nappies.' She couldn't take his children to the other side of the world. Could she? *Would* she?

Her smile did nothing to lift the chill settling over him. 'How often do you think you're going to be doing that? You'll be at work all day, dashing back to the hospital to check on a patient even when you do come home. Get real, Kristof. We're not going to be playing happy families. It might start out all right, but what happens when you've got a girlfriend in tow? Is she going to want to be second fiddle to bottles and potties?'

Go for the throat, why don't you? 'I don't have girlfriends. Only occasional enjoyable flings. Nothing permanent.' The words were out before he'd thought them through. 'As we had,' he added as his brain scrambled to rectify his blunder, only making things worse.

'There you go. A fling. Not a relationship. Not a lifelong commitment.' Alesha tossed the cover away and her feet hit the carpet.

'This is different. We've got a lifetime commitment.' It felt as if they were going round and round with neither one of them saying *exactly* what needed to be said. Standing up, he reached out, placed his hands on her shoulders. 'Alesha, look at me.'

Instantly her face lifted and those big, sad eyes locked on him. 'Yes?'

'Marry me.' The words were out before he knew he was going to say them.

Take them back. Can't. Won't. I don't want to marry again, especially when there's no love between us.

Something like a rock nudged him. Wasn't there? No, of course not.

'Say that again,' Alesha demanded.

'It makes sense. That way we can make this work as a proper family. We'll get a bigger house with space for the children and our own rooms that the kids can go between as they want.'

All colour drained from her face. 'I…' Gulp. 'That's not a marriage. That's a contract to keep the kids happy, except they won't be when they realise their parents don't share a life like their friends' parents do.'

'I thought we were trying to come to a workable arrangement where the children will be safe and happy.' Got it wrong again?

'You seem to have forgotten your reaction to that idea the night I told you I was pregnant.'

No, he hadn't. He'd had to time to weigh it all up and see there were positives about being married in this situation.

Nothing to do with loving Alesha?

He did not love her. Did he?

Sure this feeling of being turned inside out by Alesha isn't love?

It couldn't be. He'd been in love once, and that had been different.

Yeah, and she turned out to be the wrong woman for you.

What if he did love Alesha? Was in denial about it? His heart slowed as that thought took up residence in his head. No. That wasn't possible. He'd feel different, light, happy, excited. Not worried and concerned for Alesha and the babies, not trying to get everything right for them all. No, he'd be leaping in, boots and all, and to hell with the consequences. Wouldn't he?

Bending down, she picked up her bag from the floor and headed for the door. 'I know you really care about these babies, and maybe even me, but I do not want to add a half-hearted marriage into the mix.' In the kitchen she slipped her feet into her shoes. 'Thank you for the offer, but it's a no from me.'

His heart returned to his toes, and it had only just managed to climb up from there.

I want this.

Shock jerked him backwards. To have Alesha as his wife. In his life. All the time. 'Would you at least think about it?'

She paused, cupped his cheek with her palm. And sent shivers of need rattling through him. 'Thank you for asking. I know it means a lot to you, but it isn't right for us.'

Even in a moment like this he wanted her, could feel the desire ramping up and overtaking all else. Act on that and he was a dead man. Or an idiot, which he doubted. 'We'll leave things as they stand for now.' When her hand dropped away he wanted to snatch it up and place it back against his skin. 'I'm not pushing you into anything you don't want. It's another option, that's all.'

'An option?' She shuddered. 'I understand.' Did she say 'all too well' under her breath?

'I don't think you do.' He didn't, so why would Alesha? All he knew was he'd proposed when the idea had not been there minutes before. She'd given him a reprieve—one that he did not want now he'd put the idea out there. She was the reason he'd turned down the blatant offer one of the bridesmaids had made at the wedding two weeks ago. The woman had been hot and willing, and he'd said no, thanks. Which said more than just about anything could about his state of mind. Confused, worried, and also waking up.

I want to marry Alesha, and not for the babies' sake.

He was ready to try again. Because of Alesha and her beautiful nature, her sense of right, her fun, her—her everything. 'Alesha?'

Sadness softened her lips, dulled her eyes further. 'I'm going home, London home, that is. I need to be alone.'

'I'll give you a lift.' He wasn't taking any argument on that score. Alesha was shattered and upset. Riding a train was not on tonight.

'I appreciate the offer.' That came with a small, wry smile.

There was no understanding this woman. Seemed he could never get it right with her.

'Kristof proposed.' Alesha swallowed the lump in the back of her throat. 'I turned him down. How mad was I? I love him so much I hurt and I said no.'

It was the right thing to do.

He didn't love her, would one day come to regret it, especially when he met a woman he did want the whole commitment shebang with. Then he'd thank her for tonight.

Her stomach growled. Nothing to do with nausea though. It was hungry. The last thing she'd eaten had been hours ago in the canteen at work. Lunch had been a bread roll with salad and cheese—and a distant memory.

Padding out to the kitchen, she put a pan of water on and dropped in two eggs to poach, popped some bread into the toaster.

Somehow she'd managed to walk away from Kristof when her heart had been crying out to accept his proposal. She'd been strong. For her and the babies. They didn't need to grow up in a loveless family. Her love for Kristof overwhelmed her sometimes, it was so big and wonderful. But it hurt not to get any love back. Men had always dropped her when she got too serious about them.

Yeah, and this time was different. Kristof wants to marry me.

The toaster popped and the toast flipped onto the bench. Not waiting for it to cool, she plastered a good dollop of butter over it.

I pushed him away, just like he said I did with others.

Hardly. Other men left her, not the other way round.

Why did they back off? Why hadn't Kristof? That was easy. She was having his babies. He was a stayer, took responsibility seriously.

Look at how he wanted to buy her a place to live near his apartment so he could be there for them all. He'd always make sure she had everything she wanted.

All she wanted was for him to love her.

With a draining spoon Alesha lifted the eggs out of the water and slid them onto the toast. Any moment now her stomach was going to let her know it was kidding, it didn't want food at all, just another trip to the bathroom. A gentle rumble told her she was wrong. Food was required. Pulling a stool up to the bench, she plonked her butt down and dosed the eggs with enough salt and pepper to keep her taste buds happy.

There was something in Kristof's past that held him back. Something more than that failed marriage. Unless that was his problem and by proposing a loveless marriage he wasn't setting himself up to be hurt again. He'd said he loved his wife so it made sense his heart had been broken.

Egg yolk dripped down her chin. Wiping it away, she took another mouthful, chewed thoughtfully.

They'd both been hurt in the past. In different ways, but hurt was hurt whichever way it struck. She couldn't trust anyone to love her unconditionally. Yet she wanted to try. To give

Kristof a chance. What if it didn't work out? It was better to give their relationship a chance than never knowing.

Which was good thinking except for one thing. Two things. Two children. They'd be the ones to suffer if the marriage failed. If Kristof never fell in love with her.

They might also suffer if she didn't marry the man she loved.

She was back to the beginning again. Darn but she was sick and tired of going round and round with all this.

Sick and tired. Her stomach had behaved for hours now. Wow, things could be looking up. But there was a beat going on behind her eyes that wasn't letting up. Her eyelids were heavier than her handbag. It was time for bed.

Tomorrow might bring some answers to all the questions floating around in her skull. Fingers crossed.

Kristof went to work the next morning. What else was he supposed to do? In his office he dropped into the chair behind his desk and stared at the files neatly stacked in the centre. He didn't want to look through them. Which was a first. Nothing in that pile was urgent, or even needed his attention until Monday morning. So why was he here? It was Saturday and there were plenty of other things needing his attention at home.

He'd phoned Alesha again and again. She wasn't picking up. Asleep still? Or avoiding him? It didn't matter. The result was the same. He was lost. Unable to decide how to make her see marriage was the best idea for their situation.

'Hey, man, you're looking about as happy as a dog whose bone got stolen.' Harry dropped into the opposite chair. 'What's up?'

'Nothing.' Kristof studied the files.

'Woman trouble.'

'You think?'

Harry laughed. 'I've never seen you look so glum, like you have a problem you don't know how to fix.'

'Could mean my shower's stopped working and I can't get a plumber at short notice.' The trouble with friends was they saw too much and had no compunction over talking about it.

'This the woman you met in Dubrovnik?'

When had he told Harry about Alesha? 'If I say yes will you go away?'

'She dump you?'

Considering it was well known he didn't do relationships, where had his pal got that idea from?

It's the truth.

So? Didn't mean he had to admit it. 'Sort of.'

Zip your mouth.

'Why?'

'Who the hell knows?' He didn't. Or maybe he did have an inkling. 'She lets people get so close then pushes them away.' And that was all he was saying. Kristof stood up.

'You free to join our tribe for dinner tonight? It's your goddaughter's birthday.'

A kick in the gut wouldn't hurt half as much. Kristof swore. 'I totally forgot.'

'Which is why I figured something was wrong. We'll be seeing you, then?'

'Of course. I'll go shopping now for that bike I promised her.' That'd keep his mind busy.

'Want to ask your lady friend to join us too?'

Yes, he did, but a man could only take so many knockbacks. 'She's busy.'

'Or you don't want to risk her saying no.'

'When did you get so clever?' Kristof sank back on his chair, suddenly unable to move forward. As if he were stuck in a groove between what he had and what he wanted. 'I'm going to be a father to twins. A boy and a girl.'

'You're pulling my leg?' Harry shook his head. 'Of course you're not. Twins? Talk about playing catch-up in a big way. Man, you are in for some fun and a heap of responsibility.'

Responsibility he could do. Fun he wanted, but wasn't sure where to start.

Harry hadn't finished. 'The fun means letting go and diving right in, becoming a hands-on dad, and that's scaring the pants off you.'

Kristof didn't say a word. What was the point?

Harry's hand slapped the desktop. 'Duh, how stupid of me. That's not the problem. It's the kids' mother putting that sour look on your face. You are worried about letting your feelings show, or how to act on them.'

Knew he'd get there in the end. 'So?'

'So take a chance. Stop hiding from the past. Go risk your heart for them all. I am right in presuming you love her?'

Kristof froze. Couldn't have blinked if he'd tried. Love Alesha? He cared for her, a lot. Wanted what was best for her. Needed to protect her, look out for her. But love her? Crack. A sharp pain stabbed his heart. Another crack opened it further.

Was this love? This all-encompassing, debilitating sensation filling his chest was the real deal? It wouldn't go away because he expected it to? Another stab hit his chest. 'I have totally screwed up,' he admitted.

Harry stood up. 'Then go fix it.'

'What if I'm too late?' Agony lanced him. Alesha had to give him a second chance. She just had to.

'I'll tell Katie you won't be there for her party for a very good reason. But, man, you'd better deliver on this. No one gets these chances very often. Don't wreck it before you've crawled on bare knees across hot, sharp coals.'

'Thanks.'

The door closed with a resounding click and Kristof stared at the paintwork. Katie's birthday and he'd forgotten all about it. What sort of godfather did that make him? The uninvolved kind. The kind of father he'd been hoping to avoid becoming. Leaping to his feet, he made for the door, hauled it back so hard it slammed the wall. 'Harry? If it's all right with you I'll pick Katie up after lunch and take her to choose her own bike. We'll have time together.'

Harry started back towards him, a smile on his dial. 'Now you're talking like a real godfather. What about your woman? Don't waste time there, either.'

'Alesha. Her name's Alesha.' His lungs expanded. 'I'm going to see if she likes buying bikes and having dinner with strangers.' And if she didn't, he'd call tomorrow and see if she wanted to go to the farmers' market. On Monday? He'd come up with something because as of now he was not giving up on winning her over.

Alesha arranged the two teddy bears, one pink and one blue, on her dresser and smiled. It didn't matter how hollowed out and sick she felt, excitement was in her belly, warming her heavy heart. She was having two babies, and, despite all the problems waving at her, she was excited.

'Hey.' Shelley stuck her head around the door. 'You've got a visitor.'

Alesha's smile fell away. There was only one person who'd be calling on her. Kristof. She didn't have a line-up of close friends who dropped in and out at the weekends. It had to be the man who continuously played havoc with her head. 'Kristof?'

Shelley nodded. 'He said you might not want to talk to him but he looks so forlorn I had to come check with you.'

'He's right. I don't want to go near him.' She wanted to rush at him, wind her arms around his waist and never let go.

'This the father of your babies?'

It'd become impossible to keep her pregnancy a secret here when she was being sick so often. 'Yes.'

'Then what are you waiting for? Give the guy a chance to say whatever's making him look like he ate rotten fish for breakfast.'

That description did not bring a pretty picture to Alesha's mind, but it did trip the guilt button. Shoving herself up off the edge of the bed, she growled, 'All right, then. Just to shut you up, you understand?'

Shelley surprised her by wrapping her arms around her. 'You've been miserable for days. I'm thinking the other side of that coin is standing out in our lounge, hat in hand, waiting for you. Give yourself and your babies a break. Take a chance on whatever it is he's come to offer.'

How she wanted that. More than anything. As long as it came loaded with love.

'Are you up for bicycle shopping and a family dinner?' A sombre smile highlighted Kristof's mouth. It didn't quite reach the sad eyes. Make that a sorry gaze. 'It's my goddaughter's birthday and I promised her a bike. Today I realised she needs to choose it, not old man Uncle Kristof.'

Goddaughter? He did have people close to him that he loved. Alesha looked closer. There was a struggle going on over his face.

He hadn't thought to share the experience with the girl. Until now. There was love in his eyes when he mentioned the child, love he hadn't been able to share or acknowledge out loud? What had changed? Not anything to do with her and their babies, surely? 'You'd pick a plain-coloured one while she'll want fairies or out-of-world creatures.'

'You're onto it. Want to come and watch me forget how I like being in charge of everything?'

Did she? Yes, but where would it lead? To more heartbreak? Or a settling-down time between them so they could start over on planning the future? Guess there was only one way to find out. 'Give me a minute to put my face on and grab my bag.' Only now did Alesha remember she hadn't bothered with make-up this morning, thinking no one would see her.

'You don't need any of that stuff on your skin. It's beautiful as it is.' If he hadn't sounded so genuine she'd have laughed in his face and told him to go find another woman to cajole. Ah, no, she wouldn't.

'Without make-up I feel naked.' She smiled when his eyes widened. 'Don't go there. We've got a bike to shop for.'

But as she smoothed make-up over her face her smile faded. What was this about? He didn't need her to go shopping with him and his goddaughter. So why was she being included in the trip to the mall? Hope rose. She squashed it. It came back stronger. This was going to end badly.

Or really, really well.

Out in the lounge she nodded to Kristof. 'Let's go,' she said as she held her breath.

Out on the street, he pinged the locks open then placed his hands on her shoulders to draw her close. 'I'm so sorry, Alesha. I struggle with letting those nearest and dearest know how I feel. My mother has suffered because of that. I was brought up in the stiff-upper-lip brigade. My father never showed us much love, though I believe he loved me. He probably loved Mum in his own way, not totally and solely, but enough to be furious when she left him.' He paused and looked skyward. His Adam's apple bobbed. Then he locked those beautiful eyes on her. 'What I'm trying to say…' Swallow. 'I want to tell you that I love you. I've taken for ever to come round to believing it, but it is true. I love you with all my heart, Alesha Milligan. Will you share my life? Raise our babies together in a loving way?'

She gasped. Her head was light. While behind her ribs there was a lot of pounding going on. Kristof loved her? As she loved him? Looking into those blue-grey eyes she saw nothing but love, genuine, deep love—for her. Oh, my. She gasped again. Was this really happening to *her*? Had she finally found what she'd been looking for all her life? She loved him so much, and this love was like nothing she'd thought possible. It meant everything, was all-encompassing.

He cleared his throat. 'Alesha?' Fear tripped through his gaze.

'Kristof, I'm—' She stopped. About to say sorry, which he'd have taken the wrong way. 'Yes,' she said quickly to dispel his fear. He had put his heart on the line without knowing how she really felt. It was probably obvious, written all over her face when she wasn't disagreeing with him. Kristof needed to hear those words as much as she had. Rising on her toes and placing a hand on his cheek, she answered, 'I love you, Kristof. It's the for ever kind of love. The "dealing with everything that life throws at us" love.'

Relief and love rose in his eyes. 'I know there are lots of things still to work out.'

'I think we've just made that easier.' She smiled with everything that was in her heart before her mouth found his.

Kristof pulled her close, his hands holding

her waist, his mouth owning hers. 'I love you
so much it hurts,' he growled against her lips.

'I like that.' She kissed him back.

As the kiss deepened, Alesha sank in closer
and closer to that hard, caring, sexy body of
her man, and let her heart believe what it had
heard, felt everything right itself inside.

*Hey, babies, looks like we've got ourselves
a loving future.*

Kristof pulled back only enough to stare into
her eyes. 'So will you marry me now? For love
and family and all the wonderful things we
both want?'

A phone ringing broke into the moment. Annoyance and humour warred on his face as his
hand shoved into his pocket.

'Yes,' Alesha said. 'I will marry you.'

His hand hesitated as he leaned in for another kiss. 'Thank you. You've just made me
the happiest man ever.'

'You'd better answer that call. It could be
important.' As happiness expanded throughout she couldn't even find the smallest grudge
against whoever had interrupted her most important moment. If she let that happen she'd
never be fully happy.

'Hey, Katie, we're on our way to pick you
up. I'm running late but it is for the best reason.

See you in a little while, okay?' Kristof listened to his goddaughter with love in his eyes.

Love for Katie? For her? For both of them? What did it matter? He had more than enough to go around, and now that he recognised it there'd be more where he found that. Alesha snuggled against her man and waited for him to finish the call. They were going out, on a date that included a little girl, and later to a dinner with Kristof's friends. Yes, it was all coming together nicely.

On the way back to Kristof's home late that night Alesha was suddenly enveloped with sadness and a fierce longing for *everything* to be made right in her life. Possibly she was asking too much but she had to try.

'What's up?' Kristof asked as he parked in the garage.

See? The man could read her too easily. 'I need to tell my parents we're getting married.'

He turned and took her hands in his. 'You do. And if you don't get the reaction you're obviously hoping for, then remember I'm here, that I'll love you more than enough for everyone.'

Right then her heart melted, the last little doubt that he might not love her enough for long enough dissolving into the pool lying behind her ribs. 'I know.'

The follow-up kiss was tender, filled with love, and with the acceptance they had finally got it right. What one week could do to change her life was beyond description.

When they went inside Kristof led her to the lounge and sat down on the couch, pulling her onto his thighs. 'My father was my hero when I was growing up. He could do no wrong, and when my mother was sad, or angry with him, I blamed her for not loving him enough, blamed her for their marriage bust-up.' He swallowed hard. 'Then my father died and the truth came out. He'd cheated on her throughout their marriage. A lot of what he'd taught me about being a man was a lie.'

Now she understood those dark moments. 'You feel guilty for how you treated your mother.'

Kristof nodded. 'I married someone like my father in the fidelity stakes. That undermined my ability to believe in my feelings, my love. Which is why I became so focused on medicine where I knew I was good and couldn't be hurt by other people taking advantage of my feelings.'

'Pull the other one, Kristof. You think all those weeks you've spent helping out at the

Croatian children's home wasn't about showing how you felt for your mother?'

His smile, when it came, was the most relaxed and happy he'd ever given her. 'Now I
understand why I love you so much. There's
no hiding anything from you.' He kissed her,
which led to making love on the couch, and
then heading for the bedroom to fall asleep in
each other's arms.

As her eyes drooped shut Alesha whispered,
'I never knew I could be so happy. I love you.'

EPILOGUE

EIGHT WEEKS LATER Alesha walked up the pathway of the beautifully manicured gardens to the wedding venue.

Katie proudly strode ahead, a basket of rose petals in her hands, ready to sprinkle across the lawn right up to the marriage celebrant.

Alesha gripped a small bunch of peonies, the rose-pink colour lovely against her cream wedding gown that fitted tight over her breasts, and gathered over the babies tucked inside. Her face was split wide with a smile solely for the man who'd given her so much already. Yet tears streamed down her cheeks. Seemed that once she'd learned to cry she couldn't unlearn it.

She walked alone, but she wasn't alone. The people who mattered the most were here, smiling and rejoicing in her and Kristof's occasion. Cherry and Shelley had offered to walk her up the short path, but she'd declined. She didn't want to be given away—by anyone. She was going to Kristof, to be his wife and partner and lover. She was not giving herself to him to the point she didn't recognise herself again.

During the three phone calls she'd had with her parents her father had hesitatingly suggested he might give her away. She did not want that either. They had a long way to go to fix their relationship, if they ever could. As it happened her parents hadn't been able to get here for the wedding since her mother had fallen and broken her hip. They were all talking, and trying to move forward. It would be a long journey, but at least they'd started.

As she passed Antonija she saw her soon-to-be mother-in-law also crying, along with an enormous smile. Little Capeka watched solemnly from beside her adoptive grandmother. For a while Kristof and Alesha had considered bringing her to London for a new start in life, but she was struggling to find her feet and it had been decided the little girl should stay in Dubrovnik for now, at least, and, as no one had come forward to claim her, Antonija had taken her into her home permanently.

Glancing around, Alesha saw Harry's wife blink and surreptitiously wipe her eyes. What was with all these tears? It was the happiest day of her life and everyone was crying. Suddenly a laugh rippled out of Alesha's throat. Happy tears were afloat everywhere. 'This is wonderful. I am so happy to be marrying the man of my heart.' And she stepped up beside him. Kristof, he was all that really mattered. With him she'd found what she'd been looking for most of her life, and he was generous with his love. That was so special she had to keep pinching herself to make sure she hadn't fallen asleep in the sun somewhere.

Then Kristof was taking her hand and kissing her cheek. Love shone out of those blue-grey eyes she adored. 'I love you, darling.'

The celebrant chuckled. 'You're getting ahead of yourself, Mr Montfort. I think I'd better get this under way quick smart.'

Kristof's words of devotion and love were a blur for Alesha, yet she felt them deep in her heart. And when it was her turn to pledge her love she saw him open up more than ever to accept her promises of love.

'I pronounce you man and wife. Kristof, now you can kiss your bride.'

Amidst laughter and lots of sweet-scented petals, Alesha reached up and kissed her husband.

* * * * *